ALMOST TRUE

We gratefully acknowledge the support of the Canada Council for the Arts and the Ontario Arts Council for our publishing program. We also acknowledge the financial support of the Government of Canada through the Canada Book Fund.

Cover artwork: Anne Virlange, "Un jour, par la fenêtre," 2014, oil on wood, 20cm x 50 cm. Website: annevirlange.com

Cover design: Val Fullard

Almost True is a work of fiction. All the characters and situations portrayed in this book are fictitious and any resemblance to persons living or dead is purely coincidental.

Library and Archives Canada Cataloguing in Publication

Rehner, Jan, author
      Almost true / Jan Rehner.

MIX
Paper from
responsible sources
FSC
www.fsc.org   FSC® C004071

(Inanna poetry & fiction series)
Issued in print and electronic formats.
ISBN 978-1-77133-505-8 (softcover).— ISBN 978-1-77133-506-5 (epub).—
ISBN 978-1-77133-507-2 (Kindle).— ISBN 978-1-77133-508-9 (pdf)

I. Title. II. Series: Inanna poetry and fiction series

PS8585.E4473A66 2018   C813'.6   C2018-901531-4
                                                C2018-901532-2

Inanna Publications and Education Inc.
210 Founders College, York University
4700 Keele Street, Toronto, Ontario, Canada M3J 1P3
Telephone: (416) 736-5356 Fax: (416) 736-5765
Email: inanna.publications@inanna.ca Website: www.inanna.ca

ALMOST TRUE

a novel

JAN REHNER

inanna poetry & fiction series

INANNA PUBLICATIONS AND EDUCATION INC.
TORONTO, CANADA

For the gift of friendship:
Margaret, Dianne, Fran, Ms. Leigh,
Merlin, Marla, Vicky, Heather, Barbara.
And in loving memory of
Trish Swanson.

MADELEINE

OF ALL THE STORIES IN THE VERNOUX FAMILY, Madeleine's favourite was of her great grandmother Marie, who was so extraordinarily ugly that her face made painters weep and dogs slink away as if they'd been threatened with a stick. Her eyes were misaligned, her mouth askew, her skin chalky, and her hair as thin and pale as cobwebs.

Doomed to wretched loneliness, Marie wandered the shadows of the forest, while other girls her age danced in circles of bright light, amusing themselves with waltzes and handsome, clumsy boys. By the time she was sixteen, Marie knew that owls would never nest in a tree that had been struck by lightning, that stinging nettles grew best on waste ground, and that she would never marry. Eventually, her grieving father built her a rough cottage in the forest on the ridge high over the vineyards and far from the cruel tongues of the village. Her mother fashioned a thick veil, layer upon layer of delicate lace, violet-grey, the colour of sorrow, to hide her daughter's ghastly features and Marie fell under the spell of dark forest magic.

From the deer, she learned how best to hide, venturing near the fringes of the village for food only when the light melted from the sky. She learned that the pale lemon flowers of evening primrose could soothe her dry, flaking skin, and that marigold petals could cure headaches and hasten the healing of cuts and bruises. She knew every tree, even at midnight, just by touching its bark, and every plant by its colour and smell.

As time passed, she visited the edges of the village less and less, slipping easily out of people's minds and into their stories. Sometimes a hunter would glimpse her in the dusk and return with tales of an unearthly ghoul floating among the trees. Some whispered Marie had become a witch, carrying bouquets of curses in her flower basket.

And the story might have ended there but for fate, both undeniable and strange. One lonesome night, as Marie wandered her favourite paths in the forest, she saw a white horse standing perfectly still, flanks gleaming in the moonlight. And beside the shining horse, one broken man lying on the path, scarcely breathing.

Marie approached him quietly, seeming barely to touch the earth. She listened to his laboured breathing. With her small hands, she felt the pain pulsing inside him. Then she retreated into the scented darkness to gather her herbs. She prepared a poultice of comfrey to heal his wounds and knit his bones. She brewed a sedative from the dried leaves of jimson weed to ease his pain and stuffed a pillow with the dried flowers of Lady's bedstraw to mend his aching head. She gave him everything the forest had taught her, every secret, every tonic, every boon. If fate chose to give her a man, she would let him be given.

A year passed, three hundred and sixty-five midnights, while the man grew stronger and grew to love the woman in the veil with her kind hands and hushed voice that spoke to him so tenderly. He learned how to touch her and one night while he slept, she slipped away to the meadow where the deer nested and birthed a child, a little boy as soft and light as a baby bird.

Marie had lived for many years without once seeing her own face. Now she trembled in every limb for fear that she would see it replicated in her infant son. But fear surrendered to tenderness. She reached for him and turned him gently to her breast. She stared into his eyes, transfixed, until a fog clouded her gaze and life faded from her body without a sound.

The man found her the next morning with the child still cradled in her arms. An early rain had left the forest dripping and shining, a pale mist rising from its floor. But the man believed the trees themselves were crying. No birds sang and not a creature stirred, as he mounted his horse, his son folded under one arm, his lost love in the other. As he rode to the village, masses of dog roses bloomed all along the forest paths.

The villagers stared. They dropped their tools and their jaws. Little children pointed and cried aloud to see the witch of their bedtime stories abroad in the daylight. By the time the man reached the church, he was surrounded. Marie's parents, old and crooked now, pushed forward, terrified that their poor daughter's body would be ripped apart by the agitation of the pressing crowd.

"Take her away," the people shouted. "She will curse the land. She's a monster, not one of us."

"Here is your monster," the man shouted back, and with one swift gesture he ripped away the violet-grey veil.

The villagers cried out and fell back as if blinded by a brutal light.

They rubbed their eyes and couldn't believe what they saw, and rubbed their eyes again. The lustrous hair, the delicate arch of the eyebrows, the symmetry of facial bones, the soft fullness of the rose-red lips: Marie's beauty filled the square and resonated through the bright air like bells on Christmas morning.

From that day forward, all the villagers swore they had been touched by a miracle and when they prayed to the statue of Our Lady of the Vines who watched over them from high on the ridge of the forest, they swore that the Madonna's eyes were the eyes of Marie, that her pearl skin was Marie's skin, and that the perfection of the Madonna's features was duplicated in every way in the face of Marie.

"Is it true, Papa?" Madeleine always asked.

"Even untrue stories hold a hidden truth, if you are willing to hear it."

"Like a miracle, right Papa?"

"Something like that, if you believe enough."

AFTER MANY DAYS OF PRAYING, Madame Vernoux gave birth to Madeleine in the fickle month of March in the year 1923, when storm winds rattled the windows. Some of the oldest villagers distrusted March as the most perilous, most unpredictable season. Children born in March, they claimed, shared the same curious and unsettling traits as that liminal month caught between the snowy white of February and the pale green of April.

As a child, Madeleine was a March lamb. She was full of light and smiles, never sulky and seldom disobedient. She set about her chores dutifully, said her prayers, and went to mass every Sunday, though she was more likely to find godliness amid the wild roses, or drifting in on a spring breeze. She was kind, caring of others, and slow to take offence. Yet, even then, her parents despaired for their daughter's future, for Madeleine Vernoux was a perpetual daydreamer. She simply was not grounded in the real world.

She would spend hours in the family garden perched among the branches of one of the fruit trees, listening to the leaves murmuring in the breeze, imagining how apples or cherries might sound if only they could talk. Her brain refused to follow the straight lines of logic, but wandered instead among the twists and turns of wonder.

At bedtimes, her mama never bothered to read her stories, for Madeleine would imagine her own worlds, bright landscapes filled with stars and birds, or vast underwater cities that seemed to dissolve the bedroom walls and invite in the sky. When Madeleine's mother tried to describe her daughter, she would think of clouds, something far away and inaccessible.

"I don't know what to do with her," Mama said.

"Send her to school," Papa said.

But in the schoolhouse in the tiny village of Volnay in Burgundy, Madeleine drew beautiful pictures of plumed birds and winged dragons in her workbooks. Numbers and dates tumbled about aimlessly in her head. Countries shifted position and slid around the globe before her eyes. Asia traded places with Africa. Canada was another world, as fabulous as Atlantis. Rivers were blue hair ribbons, and Germany was the shape of a cauliflower. Words somersaulted across the page when she tried to read.

The teacher tried to scold her, but could never stay cross with her for long because Madeleine always did her best to please. Some of the village children taunted her, some of them relentlessly, but Madeleine would just shake her head and forgive them. Soon she had a circle of protectors, and eventually even the bullies were shamed by Madeleine's goodness.

But in the spring of 1942, in the dark days of France's humiliation and occupation, Madeleine was brimming with impossible questions: *Why are the German soldiers cross all the time? Why don't they bend their knees when they march? Why do they steal our food? Why don't they go home?*

"She's going to get into trouble," the teacher said. "I don't know what to do with her."

Papa knew the teacher was right. Madeleine loved walking in the forest or the fields at twilight and had little sense of passing time. When the Germans decreed a curfew in Volnay, she thought it a brutal act against the tranquility of the night. More than once, she wandered off and Papa had to sneak her home.

"Let's put her to work," Papa said.

So Madeleine went to work in her Papa's laundry that faced the village square, ironing sheets because they were the easiest to manage. But as she pushed and pulled the heavy iron across swathes of white linen, she dreamed of distant snow-covered fields or gliding swans, sprays of mimosa or frozen rivers that might lead anywhere, perhaps all the way to Paris. After only

a few weeks, the unmistakable odour of scorched material
alarmed customers entering the laundry.

"I don't know what to do with her," Papa said.

"Marry her off," Mama said.

"She's only seventeen."

"So? I married you at nineteen, and there'll be time for
courting."

Two suitors immediately came forward. Gaston Latour
shared a small but fine vineyard with an older brother and
sister, not on the fabled slopes of the Burgundy *grands crus*,
but on the lower slopes close by. Once one of the bullies
Madeleine had shamed in the schoolyard, Gaston Latour had
long admired her beauty. Her appearance set her apart from
her dark-eyed, dark-haired playmates. Madeleine was tall and
slim, pale-skinned, with delicate, slightly angular features. Her
eyes were a startling green, and her long hair, which curled
in the steam of the laundry, had the golden-red sheen of ripe
peaches. Gaston was handsome and hungry for her. Madeleine
scarcely noticed him. She floated by him like a breath of air,
impervious to his presence.

Armand Valleray was as poor as the proverbial mice. His
father had died too young, his lungs choked and scarred by
the trench gases of the last war that had ravaged the countryside, leaving a million and a half Frenchmen dead and leaving
Armand's mother bereft and alone, working long hours in the
laundry of Madeleine's papa to feed her small son. Armand
was devoted to his mother, determined to become a great man
she could point to as the shining worth of all her sacrifices.
He watched her carefully from the corner of his eyes, rushing
to bring her a glass of water before she knew she was thirsty,
and brushing her hair for her when her arms were too weary
to lift a comb. He often visited his mother in the laundry at
lunchtime, and it was there he first saw Madeleine.

He was transfixed by her. Amid the steam hissing from the
irons, her skin glowed. Her skin was so translucent he felt he

could see right through to her heart. He was awash with desire. Armand Valleray was nineteen and had never been in love. He studied hard at school, reading the French classics: Voltaire, Rousseau, Balzac, and Proust. For now, he tried to curb his restlessness by working in the vineyards that defined Burgundy, but when the war ended, as surely it must someday, he meant to make something of himself. He never bothered with girls. He was solitary, dedicated to ideas, to poetry, and to God. His thin, narrow face under dark brows had a natural intensity to it. He was utterly unprepared for Madeleine.

After seeing her for the first time, he forgot all about God and the vineyard, lingered in the village square, and followed her home. He hoped she might turn around and notice him. When the green door of her stone house closed behind her and she disappeared from his view, he felt a door had slammed shut on his future.

Dejected and miserable, he wandered back to the village café and tried to forget his foolishness in a glass of red wine. He reproached himself for failing Monsieur Drouhin at the Château de Pommard. The next day, he would work twice as hard in the vineyard and beg his pardon. What would happen to his mother if he lost his job? Already Maréchal Pétain and his collaborationist government in Vichy had decreed that married women could not work, and even widows were at risk of being banned from employment. He, Armand Valleray, had grave responsibilities.

"Pardon me, Monsieur."

Armand lifted his head, certain he had heard music. He gazed into Madeleine's green eyes, unable to speak.

"Why did you follow me home? Is it something to do with your mother?"

"No, I mean, yes, I followed you. Nothing to do with my mother."

"I see," Madeleine paused for a moment, taking in the tumble of dark curls falling across Armand's forehead, the tremble in his voice, the blue workman's jacket threadbare at the elbows. "Would you like to go for a walk?" she asked finally.

Armand leapt to his feet almost toppling over his wooden chair. His back was as straight as a sword as, without thinking, he held out his hand. Madeleine took it in hers, her fingers sliding between his, remarking how neatly their two hands fit together.

That afternoon, and the following afternoons for two weeks, rain or shine, Madeleine and Armand walked in the forest or fields around Volnay. The blossoms of the fruit trees fell about them like a white curtain. They waded in the clean, green water of rushing streams and let their bare feet dry in the sun. They traded the triumphant and ignominious exploits of their childhoods and the emerging shapes of their futures.

"What will you become?" Madeleine asked.

"Someone important. Someone to be respected."

Madeleine laughed and leaned back on the grassy bank of the stream with all the languor of a relaxed cat.

"You could become a famous general," she teased, "and use all your power to rid us of these Germans. Or you could be a masked bandit terrorizing the countryside, like the wolves of Burgundy in olden times. The old folk say that when the wind howls down the chimney, the wolves are on the prowl again."

Armand smiled at her stories and kissed the inside of her wrist. Light shining through the leaves of the trees dappled her with sparks of gold. He didn't know how to explain to this dazzling blaze of a girl that his ambitions, however insubstantial, were still serious. For her part, Madeleine believed he would always know her completely, even if no other man ever did.

One especially warm and soft evening when the light was golden, they lingered in the forest long past curfew. When they were together there was no one else in the world. They shared the carelessness of young lovers, the intensity of not caring what happens next. They leaned against each other and watched the sky change colour, while fireflies careened through the dusk.

Later, in the deep dark woods, they undressed each other, touched each other everywhere, memorized each other's skin. Madeleine held Armand's dark head against her breast, felt the heat of his tongue on her nipples, felt her bones melt as his mouth travelled across her stomach, down to the wetness between her legs. They sank to their knees together. Armand stretched her out in the moonlight, fearing he would crush her under his weight. She pulled him closer, arched her back and pulled him inside, kissing his shoulders, strong from his work in the fields, kissing his neck, and whispering into his ear. "Marry me," she said.

"I will love you all the days of my life," he promised.

They felt their spirits were expanding, that they had given themselves to each other in some mysterious dimension. They stayed out all night, holding tight to their vows and each other, until the sun began to rise through the morning mist. They walked straight to Madeleine's house, pure of heart, their steps light, their faces aglow with glad news to share.

"Never," said Mama and Papa in unison. The affair had moved along too quickly. Madeleine was too young, after all. Who was this Armand, and what sort of future could he promise their daughter?

Though Madeleine and Armand had been oblivious to Volnay during their courtship, Volnay had not been oblivious to them. It was the sort of small village where everyone knew everyone else's business, or tried to. The stone houses were huddled together in a hollow between sloping hillsides, with a ridge of forest high above, and a sweep of vines all around and below. The map of Volnay was a circle with a square in the centre and four spokes radiating outwards. Each spoke was a road and each road was muddy in the spring, dusty in the summer, busy during the harvest, and mostly empty in the winter. Those villagers, who did not live in the centre square, lived on one of the four roads. There was a doctor, a priest, a butcher, a baker, a two-room *mairie*, a laundry, and a café.

The village did not need anything more: the walled city of Beaune was close by and Volnay was fed by the land, by the vine-covered slopes which embraced it on all sides, and by the oak, beech, and pine forest on the high ridges filled with game.

In fact, Volnay would have been indistinguishable from many other Burgundian villages but for three things. Its stone-carved Virgin, Our Lady of the Vines, stood on a white pedestal high up on the hillsides, so high that the Virgin's crowned head rose above the tallest trees of the forest. Volnay also had a pond in the village square, the folly of a previous mayor and, finally, Volnay had Madeleine, beautiful as the first bird at dawn, whose every erratic move was duly noted, especially when those movements included a young man.

"How could you do such a thing?" cried Armand's mother. "You have shamed me before Monsieur Vernoux. Suppose I lose my job? Wake up. Look around you. Those Germans are already eyeing strong young Frenchmen to work in their factories, and you risk your job, your future, *our* future, to scratch an itch."

"It's not like that," Armand protested. "Madeleine is beautiful."

"She's the village idiot, son. I don't care how pretty she is."

The next day, Monsieur Drouhin from the Château de Pommard, who was exceedingly fond of Armand, asked him to help deliver a shipment of wines to Paris. He hoped the boy would forgive him when he learned he wasn't coming back.

MADELEINE VERNOUX'S LIFE CHANGED. She wouldn't speak to her mama. She wouldn't even look at her papa. She stayed in her room with the pale wallpaper of cream and blue stripes, tracing over and over again the perfect, full lips that Armand had kissed.

"Come out, Madeleine," Mama begged. "You have a good heart, but you must come down to earth. You can't float through life."

Madeleine knew too well the truth of her mama's words. Her carefree world was shattered. Where once there was only lightness, there was now only heaviness, a burdensome weight anchoring her firmly to the ground. Colours were muted. Where once she had lived in a green world—the spring-green of the sloping hills, the emerald-green of the leafy vines, the thick, green-black of the forest—now she saw only the dull browns of the village, the dusty and chalky shades of the earth, the slates and blacks of the roofs, and the stone walls that marked out the borders of the famed *domaines*.

She waited for Armand to return. She waited for many days, and then she waited some more. As the days slipped into weeks and the weeks into months, and still he did not come, she felt something at the back of her throat that hurt. He was like smoke, swirling in the air she breathed, drifting under her clothes, clinging to her skin. She smelled like burning leaves.

Mama did her best to intercede, coaxing her from her room and sending her to the village shops with the ration books. But when Madeleine wandered among the market stalls, she heard whispers and laughter that had never reached her ears before. Her gentle lunacy had always shielded her from prejudices and jealousies. Now she was exposed to barbed words, unable to understand in the watery maze of her mind what she might have done to offend people. She was helpless as a bird with broken wings.

In her misery, Madeleine found one true friend, Léa Legard, the village doctor's daughter. Motherless since infancy, Léa could not bear cruelties or gossip and she rushed to Madeleine's defence, just as she had when they were both children in the schoolyard. When she was a little girl, Léa had thought of Madeleine as a sort of misplaced saint, or maybe the queen of another country that was too far away to visit. Now, at the wise old age of eighteen, she could see clearly that Madeleine was simply broken-hearted.

Having diagnosed the problem, Léa set about finding the cure. She was more than a little cross with Armand Valleray. It was one thing to cause a scandal, but quite another to vanish from Volnay and leave Madeleine to face alone the fluttering tongues of the villagers, and the salacious glances of Gaston Latour. So Léa saddled her old faithful horse and rode to the neighbouring Château de Pommard.

The honey-coloured château was a landmark of the Burgundy region, surrounded by an elaborate garden and by twenty hectares of prime vines, most enclosed within stone walls with high-arched gates of wrought iron. Léa had heard the stories of how the soldiers had shuffled the family off into an adjacent farmhouse, claiming the light-filled rooms of the château for themselves. They turned the beautiful ground-floor salons into an ammunition depot, even chopping wood on the marble floors and scarring them permanently. Her anger kept the fear from her eyes when the German patrol stopped her at the start of the long drive up to the grand house and the fields beyond.

"Name," the soldier snapped.

Léa threw him a fierce scowl and handed over her identity papers, but he only laughed at her dark looks and the blush on her cheeks.

"Léa Legard." He pronounced the name with flair, as if showing off his recently learned French. "Business?"

Léa was tempted to say *my own*, but cast aside that reply as too provocative. She answered civilly. "I've come to see Monsieur Drouhin. An urgent message from my father, Dr. Legard."

Her voice was steady even as she told her lie and the soldier waved her forward.

Drouhin was surprised to see her, though he knew perfectly well who she was. Everyone knew the widowed doctor's daughter with her long black braid, and her rosy round cheeks.

"I've come about Armand," Léa said.

"Ah," said Drouhin. "Then you'd better have some wine."

IN THE WEEKS AFTER HER VISIT to the Château de Pommard, Léa suffered under the burden of secrets. The price of Monsieur Drouhin's information had been her vow of silence. Now her heart ached for Madeleine, and raged against the treachery of men. As a distraction, she introduced Madeleine into her small circle of friends. Eugénie Latour, Gaston's sister, was the first to accept Léa's invitation to a Sunday picnic.

Eugénie's story was one of tragedy and fierce determination. Her parents had died within weeks of each other, victims of the Spanish flu that had swept through France with a swiftness that rivalled the German army's. Eugénie had found comfort in the affection of her twin brother, Julien, and together they vowed to maintain the five hectares of vines their parents had been so proud of. Eugénie tried to be a mother to little Gaston, but he was headstrong and unruly, given to temper tantrums and sullen pouts. He resented the closeness of the twins. Even as Eugénie, tender-hearted, tried to pull him closer, he pushed her away. That tug of war left them both exhausted.

When France declared war on Germany, Eugénie despaired. She knew that Julien had the soul of a soldier, just waiting to be ignited. He enlisted immediately, and when the Germans swept around and over the Maginot Line like angels of death, Julien was taken prisoner. Eugénie wrote to him almost every day, while every day Gaston grew wilder, a stranger in his own home.

Now Eugénie spent long days alone, struggling to maintain the family vineyard. That weight on her shoulders, together with her square face and high smooth brow, made her seem older, but Eugénie was still a young woman. When she was invited to the picnic, she said yes because she longed for a bit of pleasure. She was also curious about Madeleine, only vaguely remembering her from school as a sweet, wayward child. She knew, but could scarcely believe, that Gaston was besotted with Madeleine for he was too vain and too greedy to be satisfied by a single girl—usually he flirted and then pushed girls away, just as he pushed away his plate after eating.

Léa's other friend was Simone Benoir who loved parties and had a laugh like water rushing over stones. She had an oval, fine-featured face with darting, teasing black eyes. Her entire family—parents, aunts, uncles and cousins—had fled Paris a few months before the Germans marched into the city in June 1940. Her grandfather had made a fortune in the late 1800s as a famous *négociant*, so it was natural for the family to resettle in the wine country of Burgundy. But Simone often found the pace of life in Volnay exasperatingly slow. She missed Paris, the chestnut trees and the ice-cream stand by the Île Saint-Louis, the wide boulevards and the pink light, the slick green sidewalks after a rain. If she were still in Paris, she might not have agreed to socialize with the daughter of a laundry man, but she couldn't wait to meet Madeleine, the heroine of so many scandalous whispers.

They all met in Léa's back garden that smelled of verbena and lavender. There was a blue tablecloth, a pitcher of lemonade and a plate of strawberries. Eugénie brought a bottle of pale yellow wine and Simone amazed everyone by supplying *chambertine*, a Burgundian cheese, to go with the baguettes.

"Where did you get that?" Léa exclaimed. Rationing was strict in Volnay. It seemed that only Germans were allowed cream and cheese.

Simone smiled slyly and didn't answer the question. She was staring at Madeleine who was looking virginal in a white dress flecked with tiny pink flowers. She was holding a small book of poetry on her lap, and she looked like a painting by Renoir that Simone had once seen in Paris. Apart from a quick, shy smile when introduced, Madeleine didn't seem interested in Simone or her cheese. She turned the pages of her book slowly, seeming to occupy an inviolate space.

Léa hugged Eugénie and asked after Julien. She turned to Madeleine and explained that Julien was a prisoner of war.

Madeleine raised her eyebrows. "A prisoner?"

"Yes, he was captured in one of the first battles and marched for miles and miles to an officer's camp in Silesia. The conditions are pretty grim, but at least he's alive."

Madeleine closed her book. "How terrible," she whispered in an impassioned voice, "to be shut away, to be torn from your real life and forced to live a ghost life."

She placed her hand over Eugénie's and her green eyes glittered with tears. A shiver travelled the length of Eugénie's body. It felt as if Madeleine were speaking for Julien, that for a moment he had taken possession of Madeleine's body and spoken directly to his sister with Madeleine's voice. She felt something in her breaking. She pulled her fingers away and poured the wine with trembling hands.

When the afternoon ended, Eugénie still felt shaken and she took Simone's arm as they turned into the lane in front of the doctor's house while Léa waved goodbye. Simone leaned in close.

"She's just as daft as people say," Simone sniffed.

Eugénie just stared at the ground. She felt she had peered into another dimension, and that, in the face of a beautiful, distraught young woman, she had read the fate of both of her brothers.

IN THE FALL OF 1942, while Léa tried to rescue Madeleine from her sorrow, Burgundy grew restless under the yoke of occupation. The German army was systematically stripping the country bare: wheat from the Île de France, vegetables and fish from Provence, apples from the orchards of Normandy, Charolais beef from Burgundy and, most of all, trainload after trainload of wine, thousands and thousands of bottles of wine.

The *vignerons* suffered a double loss; not only were their finest wines requisitioned to fill glasses across the Rhine, but their means of making new wines were severely reduced. Sugar for the wine was scarce. Egg whites, used to clarify the wine, were even scarcer. Chemical fertilizers were practically non-existent, and rations of insecticides were inadequate. At first, there was barely enough copper sulphate to combat mildew and fungal diseases, and then there was none. Germany needed copper and other metals for its war industry and soon soldiers were scouring homes and cellars for copper wire, pipes, pots, and pans.

Once again, Madeleine asked awkward questions. If all the metal could be melted down to make guns and tanks and bullets, why couldn't the guns and tanks be melted down again to make useful things? *Oh, Madeleine,* her Mama said, which meant that would never happen. Madeleine thought men just didn't want to do it. They seemed to want weapons more than anything. She knew she would never understand the extent to which men seemed to want to kill each other.

When September came, the villagers of Volnay turned out to help the farmers harvest their grapes. The shortages had taken their toll and the harvest was half what it had been in 1940, but the tradition, as rooted in the hearts of the people of Burgundy as the vines on the hillsides, was sacred.

The people of Volnay lived and died on the land. They fashioned their metaphors from the earth and the weather. The Germans were the blistering sun that dried the soil to dust, and also the cold wind that blew it away, but even they could not alter the laws of nature. The vines had no choice in the matter. The sun shone as it always had, the ancient roots dug deep for moisture, photosynthesis worked its magic, and the Boche could do nothing about it. The grapes were ready for harvesting.

Léa and Madeleine's families volunteered to help Eugénie and Gaston Latour, in one case because Léa and Eugénie were friends, and in the other because Madeleine's mama and papa still clung to the hope that their daughter might be saved by a respectable marriage. Madeleine, suspecting nothing of her parents' schemes, braided her hair, and tucked the long plaits under a white kerchief, unwittingly making herself look more alluring than ever.

As Madeleine worked along the rows of vines, the wooden handle of the harvesting shears fitting neatly into the palm of her hand, she gave herself completely to the rhythm of the day and the perfume of the grapes. She didn't mind the constant stooping and standing, or the weight of the basket on her arm. Her small hands were dexterous and gentle, handling the grapes as if they were as precious as jewels, pale orbs of citrine and peridot. When her basket grew too heavy, she called to Léa and they walked together to the central wagon where all the pickers emptied their baskets before starting the shearing again. Mama and Papa seemed to be happy, laughing and chatting with Gaston. Madeleine waved to them as she started down another row of vines. Gaston waved back, and his eyes followed her hungrily.

At lunchtime, the villagers crowded around long tables set out under the beech trees in the courtyard. Before the days of rationing, the tables had groaned under the weight of whole hams and chickens, slabs of pâté and cheese. But Eugénie had done her best and there were bowls of rabbit stew, tomatoes and cucumber from her garden, and cherry preserves from her cellar. And wine. There was plenty of wine.

Gaston lifted his voice and his glass. "Here's to that fool Pétain, eh?" To the responding grumble, Gaston slowly tipped his glass letting the wine spill as the grumbling turned to laughter.

Eugénie watched her brother charm her friends and neighbours, the men he gambled with, the wives he flirted with. She noticed he carefully avoided the wives she suspected he slept with. Simone, who had reluctantly agreed to help in the kitchen because she was too clumsy with the vines, blushed whenever Gaston winked at her. As he circled the table, he took special care with Monsieur and Madame Vernoux, but Madeleine seemed as imperturbable as ever.

When the lunch ended, and the volunteers began to return to the vineyard, Eugénie stole a quiet moment with Léa.

"Gaston seems set upon Madeleine. Does she speak of him?"

"Not a word," Léa assured her. "But her parents, I think, would like her to settle down. They worry about her. She's never forgotten Armand nor, I suspect, has most of the village."

Three days into the harvest, something extraordinary happened, perhaps a portent of things to come. Old Jacques, the big plough horse pulling the wagon of grapes, stumbled and fell onto his side. The heavy load lurched ominously and one of the wagon's wooden shafts snapped, impaling the left haunch of the horse. Jacques made an awful choking sound, almost like a human sob.

The men came running from every direction to shore up the tipping wagon. If the load of grapes fell, the harvest would be lost.

Madeleine came running too, but she ran straight to Jacques. While the men heaved and shouted, Madeleine knelt quietly beside the horse, placing her small hand on his enormous head. Jacques' nostrils flared and he pawed the air with his great hooves, but Madeleine was oblivious to the danger and to the blood seeping into the ground, staining the hem of her dress.

She whispered into Jacques' ear. He responded with a soft nicker. Slowly, she ran her hands down his black hide, slick with sweat. The broken end of the shaft was buried in the horse's flesh. Madeleine grasped the wood in both hands, swaying a little as if to some music only she could hear. With one great pull, she yanked out the shaft, staunching the wound with her white kerchief, her cheek pressed against Jacques' side.

For a moment, time seemed to stop and motion stilled. Everyone stared at the beautiful woman with blood on her face and a huge horse in the palm of her hand. Then Madeleine whistled softly and Jacques heaved himself onto his feet.

The moment was over. The spell was broken. No one was quite sure what had happened, though everyone would remember it. Some people began to believe that Madeleine had

unearthly powers, but Léa believed her gift was simply kindness, a mysterious alchemy of touch and sound, the caress of
her hands and the music of her voice.

Finally the picking was done. It was tradition for the workers
to gather wildflowers to decorate the cart and make a bouquet
for the lady of the house. Usually, Eugénie hung the bouquet
above the entrance to the *cave* to bring good luck. This year,
she gave it to Madeleine, pulling her close.

"Gaston isn't who your parents think he is," she murmured.
"Watch out for him."

Eugénie was profoundly grateful to Madeleine for saving
both Jacques and the grapes, but her words still tasted bitter
in her mouth. It grieved her heart that she could not trust her
own brother.

IN NOVEMBER, THE WIND CHANGED. Gold leaves fell in clouds.
The Germans crossed the Demarcation Line and occupied the
entire country.

Madeleine's mama and papa hunched over their forbidden
radio and listened to the news with alarm. These were not the
same Germans who had marched into France so arrogantly.
Their invincibility had been punctured: their planes burst into
flames in the skies over England, their tanks choked in the
swirling sands of North Africa, their feet bled in the snows of
Russia. They were rattled and nervous. The fist was tightening.
More and more often, the word "Gestapo" was whispered in
Volnay. Madeleine hated even the sound of the word, beginning
with the hiss of a snake, followed by a sharp stab, ending with
an utterance of woe.

The French fought back against the German requisitions as
best they could by lying and cheating. Those with foresight
had already hidden their most exquisite wines behind hastily
constructed brick walls in their *caves*. Children were urged to
collect spiders in the hope that they would spin webs across the
bricks and so disguise their newness. Candlelight only dimly

outlined myriad passages and cobwebbed, shadowy corners. If the soldiers were brave or thirsty enough to insist on entering the gloomy *caves,* a wine grower might glance at the soldier's beautiful shiny jackboots and mutter warnings about burst pipes or the rising of the river Saône that had, sadly, flooded the cellar with muddy water.

Others hid their wine by digging deep holes in the forest, marking them with clever patterns of stones or planted shrubbery. Bottles of *vin ordinaire,* rough or young on the palate, became *grands crus* overnight with just the switch of a label. In the finest restaurants, where only German officers could afford to eat, a glorious bottle of Corton-Charlemagne could go twice as far with a funnel and some tap water.

At night, all along the railroad lines of France, farmers, wine growers, and *cheminots,* or railroad workers, were stealing back their own from railway cars loaded with goods bound for Germany. Jerry cans and rubber hoses were sometimes used to siphon all the wine from barrels destined for Berlin. When the barrels were opened, the Germans would find that the wine had been mysteriously transformed into water. Or perhaps there would be an accident along the line and several Charolais steers would escape from a smashed railway car. If a railcar door were to be left open unaccountably, a joint of pork or a sack of potatoes might easily fall out. The Germans became surly and doubled their patrols. Soon, rustling became too dangerous a sport for any but the most brazen to play.

It came as no surprise when Gaston Latour was arrested. Within hours, the village buzzed with the news.

He was caught out after curfew.
He was stealing from the train yard.
He must be part of the Resistance.
He's to be executed at dawn.

By the time the news reached Léa, it was impossible to distinguish the wildest rumours from fact. She was with Madeleine, teaching her to knit scarves and socks that could be sent to

Julien Latour in his POW camp. She tossed aside her knitting and buried her face in her hands.

Madeleine was alarmed by the change in her friend. "Léa? What is it? We all knew Gaston took too many risks."

Léa shook her head. Most people assumed that Madeleine looked at the world through a thin veil or, perhaps, a misty fog. But she was far more observant than others supposed.

"I thought you weren't interested in Gaston Latour," Léa replied.

"Oh, Léa. Let's not waste words. Why are you so upset?"

"It's the others, Maddy. Other people are involved and Gaston is not above selling them out to save his own skin."

"Then you'll have to get him out."

"It's not so simple. How am I supposed to do that?"

Madeleine smiled at her. "The Germans are very fond of wine."

"Of course, Monsieur Benoir. Come with me."

"I think Simone is uncomfortable around me."

"Well I'm not. And I need you there to give me the courage to face her father. Come on."

THE BENOIR ESTATE STRETCHED BEYOND the northern outskirts of the village, close to the fabled vines of Pommard. The pale stone house was topped with a steepled roof of multicoloured Burgundian tiles, flashing red and gold in the sun. It had walls of brindled masonry and windows of old glass that shone copper in the light. Inside, Monsieur and Madame Benoir were subdued elegance itself, sitting apart on either end of a pink chaise lounge, their faces darkened by the news of the Latour boy's plight.

Simone, flushed with the drama of the moment, sat on an ottoman at her father's side and urged him to help. "Gaston is a lovely man. He wouldn't hurt a fly."

Léa didn't agree, but kept silent.

"He owns a vineyard, doesn't he?" Monsieur Benoir inquired. "And this young woman," he gestured toward

Madeleine, "surely, Mademoiselle, you are the woman who saved the horse."

"He stumbled," Madeleine replied. "I merely helped him up."

"Oh, no, Mademoiselle. I think you did much more than that. But no matter. What would you have me do for your friend?"

"Please, sir," Léa interjected. "Simone will have told you that Eugénie's other brother is already a prisoner-of-war. Without Gaston, she will be lost. And there are others involved—"

Monsieur Benoir held up his hand to stop Léa from saying any more. He was no fool. He hadn't amassed a fortune without learning a thing or two about the people around him, and without knowing there were some things better kept in the dark. He wondered if the poor sister, Eugénie, would be so anxious to rescue her brother if she knew how much he gambled and what was often at stake.

"Where is Mademoiselle Latour?" Madame Benoir asked.

"Already at the *mairie* in Volnay," Simone answered. "Léa's father met her there at first light."

"Very well," Monsieur Benoir agreed. "I'll go along and see what I can do. Perhaps the boy's sweetheart can soften a guard's heart."

He was staring at Madeleine, but it was Simone who jumped up. "Of course, Papa. Let's go."

In the weeks that followed, Gaston appeared chastened. He was often seen walking in the company of Simone. It was rumoured that a great deal of wine had changed hands, and more than a few francs.

DECEMBER BLEW IN ON A CRUEL WIND. On the hillsides of Volnay, the roots of the vines dug deeper clinging to life, while the edges of the leaves curled up and turned black. There was a dampness in the air that sliced through clothes, skin, and bone. The wind licked up the light greedily—the days were short and grey, the nights long and inky black.

Just before Christmas, there was a mighty storm, rare for the village. The old folk saw it as yet another sign of the curse of war. Surely the wolves of Burgundy were on the prowl.

Léa was on her way to check on the Vernoux house when Madeleine emerged from a swirling cloud of snow carrying a swan.

Startled, Léa cried out. Madeleine was still wearing her nightdress, the skirt and sleeves puffed out by the wind. She looked like a bird herself, a ghost bird, an apparition. Her lips and fingers were blue.

"They're freezing to death," Léa heard Madeleine shout over the wind. "The pond is icing over and they're trapped."

Without asking or hesitating, Madeleine thrust the swan into Léa's arms and vanished behind a curtain of snow. Léa instantly stiffened. She was terrified of swans. They might have been a pretty sight gliding along in a pond, but they were spitting, hissing, biting creatures on land.

And surprisingly heavy. She stared down at the bundle of feathers in her arms, the long neck drooping towards the ground. Her only thought was to get rid of it. She trudged through the snow to the Vernoux's front door and banged on it with her foot.

Madeleine's mama screamed and then cursed, but her papa put on his coat and went out in search of his daughter.

"The pond," Léa shouted after him. "She said the swans are caught in the ice."

Madeleine's mama refused to touch the swan, so Léa kicked off her wet shoes and carried it into the living room, depositing it in a feathery heap in front of the fireplace. Immediately, the swan stretched its neck and spread its wings. Léa jumped back, terrified it would attack. But the wings folded, the neck retracted, and the swan sank to the ground.

Relieved, Léa looked around the room as she removed her coat. Two black crows were perched on a windowsill. A nondescript terrier, its right foreleg in a splint, studied her warily from underneath a table. A mangy cat with orange stripes blinked at her from its single eye.

She met the gaze of Madeleine's mama who nodded in response to the unasked question.

"It's her menagerie. She brings home anything that's hurt. It's almost as if the animals seek her out. I don't know what to do with her."

The door banged open and Léa turned to see Madeleine framed in the entrance with another swan cradled in her arms. She'd lost her shoes in the snow, her nightdress was sopping wet, clinging to her legs and torso. Her hair dripped pond water and she was shivering violently.

Her papa appeared behind her and picked her up in his arms, swan and all. "Please, Léa. Fetch your father."

By the time Dr. Legard arrived, Madeleine's mother had removed her daughter's sopping clothes, put her into a dry nightdress, and buried her under a mountain of quilts. The doctor held Madeleine's limp hand and listened to her chest. At first her breathing was harsh and uneven and then it seemed she was hardly breathing at all. She was as pale as marble and as cold as stone.

Dr. Legard tugged on the ends of his black beard, as he always did when the diagnosis was bad. "I fear she will contract pneumonia. The next few days will be critical."

Mama sat with Madeleine for hours, rubbing her hands and her limbs, trying to coax warmth back into her daughter's blood. She berated herself for every cross word she had ever spoken to her. What did it matter if a few animals cluttered up her living room? What did it matter if her daughter liked to perch in the tree in the back garden at night and count the stars? She was her own flesh and blood, her own March lamb. She piled on so many quilts that Papa was sure his daughter would suffocate before she had any chance of dying from pneumonia.

After the bone-chilling cold came a fierce blast of fever. Dr.

Legard visited again and quilts were pulled from the bed and flung into corners. Basins of ice water and soothing cloths were fetched.

Madeleine's nightdress was drenched with sweat, her hair plastered to her cheeks. Noise boomed and receded in her ears like the sea in a giant shell. Everything in her head seemed to come loose, spinning into blackness. She suffered from hallucinations where there was no gravity. Delirious, she floated high above Volnay, where the houses and people looked like children's toys. She rode on the backs of swans and talked to the wolves in their own guttural tongue. Everything was red, the air, the sun, whatever she looked at. She watched a young man walk across the fields all alone. He stopped and looked up at her as she flew by and she saw that he was crying. She called out to him but he vanished into the woods.

On the sixth day of her illness, just before dawn, yellow lines cut through the sky, but the bedroom was dark. Madeleine opened her eyes and could see nothing. *I'm blind*, she thought.

Then, she felt the soft thud of a cat landing on the mattress, and saw the beam of a single green eye glowing in the dark. The cat marched across her chest and curled up on her shoulder, its fur tickling her cheek. Madeleine was so relieved she laughed out loud. That sound was greeted by a rustling of wings from the crows on the windowsill and a bark from the pile of fur at the end of her bed.

The door to her room opened, and Papa's head leaned in.

"Where are the swans?" Madeleine asked.

"Ah," Papa said. "You're back."

Dr. Legard ordered strict bed rest for a month. "She needs plenty of nourishing food," he added, knowing even as he said it that food was almost as scarce as medicine, especially in the winter.

Mama was determined that Madeleine would recover. She made soup out of anything she could find, chicken bones and dried mushrooms and apples. She even eyed the crows. She ate less and less to give Madeleine more. And she learned how to linger by certain market stalls, willing to trade an antique clock, say, for a purloined pork chop and a rasher of bacon.

Léa visited almost every day and filled the time by reading to her. At first, Madeleine would listen to the calming rhythm of Léa's voice and fall asleep, or she would imagine the words falling all around her like soft rain. Finally, she couldn't stand it anymore.

"Léa, why aren't you talking to me? What's happening in the village?"

Léa shut the book she was reading from and forced a smile.

Her father had warned her that Madeleine was fragile, that she mustn't be upset. Léa longed to tell her what was happening in the village, but most of it was bad. She longed to break her silence and tell her what she knew about Armand, whose name Madeleine had cried out in her delirium. But Madeleine was so unpredictable, anything might happen if she knew the truth.

"The swans are back in the pond. The January thaw melted the ice. Your mother says she misses them. She'd come to think of them as ornaments decorating either side of the fireplace."

Madeleine reached for her friend's hand and squeezed it. "Dear Léa. You can't protect me. I know things in my bones. I've heard the wolves howling at night. Telling me the truth would be kinder."

Léa didn't think so, but she could see by the haunted look in Madeleine's eyes that she would not rest or heal until true words were spoken.

So Léa told her all about the black shadows cast over France that would stain the country's honour for years to come. She told her that the rumours from Paris were true, that the Jews, thousands of Jews, hundreds of children, had been rounded up in the summer like cattle and shipped to camps in Poland and Germany where they disappeared into a hail of ashes. She told her that Monsieur Rosen, the teacher who'd let Madeleine colour in her workbooks at school, had vanished. She told her of the evil scheme called *Service du travail obligatoire* that ordered men between sixteen and sixty to go to Germany to work in the war factories. Anyone who resisted or tried to escape would be hunted down and severely punished.

Frenchmen were now hunting Frenchmen: Pétain, reviled now by many for his complete toadyism, had established a police force called the Milice—their own countrymen dressed in khaki shirts, black berets, and black ties, despised and feared in equal measure.

Every dreadful syllable uttered by Léa seemed to alter Madeleine physically. Two patches of pale lilac appeared under her eyes and the eyes themselves seemed to change colour, softening from a vivid green to a sort of mossy grey.

"This terrible news will kill you," Léa whispered. "My father warned me not to speak of the war."

"No, Léa, knowing the truth is better than fearing the unknown. Better to fight real evil in the world than to cover your ears and run from it."

"And Armand. Oh, Maddy, I've known for months. Monsieur Drouhin made me promise not to tell."

Madeleine held up her hand. "Shh. Keep your promise. Armand will come back soon and tell me himself."

OF ALL THE MONTHS WHEN HE MIGHT have chosen to return, fate seemed to dictate that Armand would come home in March, that unruly month when Madeleine was born. One day, the flame azalea in Madeleine's back garden would be so covered in flowers it resembled a burning bush. The next day, after a drenching rain, the grass would be sprayed with azalea petals that resembled drops of blood.

No one understood the treachery of March better than the vintners. Sunshine one day, punishing hails the next. They stood around in groups watching the pale untrustworthy sky. *If it doesn't rain too much, if it rains enough, if there is no hail or wind—if, if, if—the harvest might be saved.*

Madeleine welcomed March with wide-open arms. After her confinement, her limbs rejoiced to be outdoors again. She loved the air after a hard rain and the spicy smell of the laurel bushes just before everything turned green. Even the light was green. Every day she walked, each day a little farther than the last. She tilted her head as if the breeze were whispering to her and heard the rumours of Armand's return.

When she felt strong enough, she walked to the forest, to the meadow where they had made their first vows of love to each other. She knew he would look for her there among the pine trees and wildflowers.

Birds heralded his coming, the sound of a pine bough swinging, and the snap of a twig under his boot. Her heart was beating fast.

She turned to greet him and his smile went straight through her. Surprise swept all over her face. She stared at him, confused. She thought she was prepared, but instead she was caught out, ambushed.

She held his gaze for as long as she could stand it. "Why?" she whispered. "Why are you wearing a cassock?"

"It's wonderful news, Madeleine, isn't it? I thought you knew. I'm to be a priest. Monsieur Drouhin arranged everything. I'm studying at a seminary in Paris."

A seminary—long silences, unadorned cloisters, the odours of incense and lilies, dark wooden benches, and acts of contrition. Madeleine sank to the ground and hugged her knees. She thought of the only two priests she knew from her own and a neighbouring village, dried sticks, both of them. To think of Armand cloistered away in a place that must surely be lonely and sparse, in a place where she could not reach him, brought her physical pain.

She stretched out her hand and after a moment's hesitation he took it, settling down on the grass beside her. She leaned her head on his shoulder, felt the sharp intake of his breath. He pulled away.

"What we did here was wrong, Madeleine. I pray that God will forgive us for our sins."

"Sins? No, Armand. We were happy. We were proud of ourselves. Love is not a sin. You've been infected by an imposter god who understands only punishment."

She couldn't have stunned him more had she slapped him. Instinctively he closed a fist around the wooden cross that now hung from his neck. It was, she thought, the gesture of a child, like crossing your fingers behind your back before telling a lie.

She listened impassively, helplessly, as Armand rattled on about his God and good works and vocations. Every word he spoke drove nails into her heart. She studied his dark pensive face, the thick black of his curls, the lips she knew the feel of on her skin. He had erased their closeness, cancelled it out, ground it into the dirt.

Something curdled inside her. She feared she might never be able to move again, that she would take root in this very spot. Her skin would turn to leather and then stone. Vines would grow over her, and birds would perch on her head and build nests in her lap.

Finally, Armand seemed to notice. "Are you all right, Madeleine?"

She remained completely silent. She had no vocabulary, no voice. She knew that any sound she tried to make would be completely inappropriate. It would be the faint mewling of a starving cat, or the frantic beating of a bat's wings stuck in a chimney. Or the piercing bay of a wolf.

"I'm sorry, Madeleine."

She couldn't look at him any longer. *I'm sorry* is what people said when things were irrevocable. With a great effort she stood up and walked away without once looking back, though she longed to do so.

A kind of wildness gripped Madeleine by the throat after that day. Her eyes smouldered and her nerve endings were on fire. She grew reckless, seeming to seek out danger. She glared at anyone who stared at her. She openly flaunted the curfew. When a young German soldier threatened her, she snarled at him like a dog.

"Leave her," the soldier's commander ordered. "She's mad."

Madeleine didn't care. Nothing could hurt her anymore. She walked alone in the forest at midnight, seeking refuge in solitary wandering and exhaustion. Darkness vibrated from her in pulsing waves. Her long hair hung in knots and tangles down her back and blew like streamers in the wind. She stumbled upon a patch of dog violets in the woods, the purple flowers symbolizing love. She knew if she touched them they would turn black.

One night near the end of March, cold and exhausted, she startled a wild boar. Its tusks curved upwards, gleaming in the moonlight, poised to slice her in two. Its breath billowed into the air; its hooves pawed the ground. Madeleine was unafraid. She was sure no animal would ever hurt her. She lifted a hand and the beast charged, veering at the last second and knocking her sideways onto the ground. The stiff bristles of its hide ripped a wide strip of skin off her right leg.

She lay where she'd been thrown for a long time, feeling her hot blood and hot tears. The boar had smelled her anger, sniffed out the blackness inside her. She had become a thing to be frightened of. The realization jarred her as much as the impact of the beast. She hoped that if she stayed still, the poison would drain from her and soak into the ground with her blood and tears.

In the red dawn, she followed the blackbirds home. She hugged her mama and begged her forgiveness. Her papa stood to the side with a hunting rifle that he'd hidden from the Germans gripped in his hands. "If you like," he said. "I'll shoot Armand through the heart."

"No need, Papa. He's done that all by himself."

She crawled to bed. Perhaps she would sleep for a hundred years and wake up consoled and pure again.

MADELEINE CARRIED HERSELF DIFFERENTLY when next she went to market. She had travelled far inside herself. She was learning to accept her solitude, trying it on as another woman might try on a new dress. People still stared, but combed and cleaned, she was more beautiful than ever, a darker beauty that made people think of shadows and lunar eclipses.

She was looking for Léa in the village, but she could not help noticing who else was not there. At the stall of the turnip man, the young son Henri was not making change. In the *boulangerie*, there was no Pierre collecting ration tickets. At the café, no Jean-Louis, no Georges.

Madeleine headed for the schoolhouse. Perhaps Léa was teaching on a Saturday, filling in as she'd promised to do for the vanished teacher, Monsieur Rosen. But when Madeleine peered through the window, the neat rows of children's desks were empty. She felt a flicker of doubt. Perhaps Léa was avoiding her. Perhaps she too was frightened of her, not able to forgive her journey into the pitch-black that was triggered by the sight of Armand in a black cassock.

When she reached Léa's house, she was relieved that Dr. Legard was happy to see her.

"Léa," he shouted. "Madeleine is back." And then, softly, "You *are* back?"

Madeleine nodded.

"Good. Stay among us this time. There's a limit to everything, even heartache."

Madeleine lowered her head, humbled that the doctor cared and ashamed that she had caused her friends even a moment of worry. Before she could even lift her head, she felt Léa's arms around her, holding her tight.

Something still hurt at the back of her throat like a sharp stone she couldn't swallow, but Madeleine was determined not to slip ever again into the quicksand of melancholy. She practiced repeating to herself all the things she loved: Mama humming in the kitchen, the smell of soap on Papa's hands, two crows that flew away on mended wings but came back to visit her, a one-eyed cat asleep on her bed, a skinny dog with a limp, one beautiful, long-ago night of love-making in the forest, unspoiled by what came after, and Léa.

THAT SUMMER OF 1943, The air felt electric and sultry. More and more young men fled into the thick forests of the Morvan, a hundred kilometers or so west of Volnay, to avoid being shipped to Germany. The ranks of the Resistance swelled with displaced, desperate men, most driven more by fear of the *Service du travail obligatoire* than by patriotism.

Those not quick enough to flee were soon arrested. The lucky ones were imprisoned at Fresnes, outside Paris. The unlucky, including Pierre, who had collected his last ration tickets at the *boulangerie,* were executed. Throughout the villages of France, gunfire at dawn from firing squads drowned out the crowing of roosters. But night was even worse than dawn, for the Gestapo were night hunters, carnivorous prowlers. The Milice merely set the traps on the Gestapo's behalf and then watched from the sidelines like ghouls at a public hanging.

For a time, young men working in the vineyards were exempt from the *Service du travail obligatoire*—wine still tasted better than blood. Pétain ordered more and still more wine to flow to Germany. To stretch dwindling supplies, he launched an anti-alcoholism crusade for the French under the guise of healthier living. He forbade bars from serving wine on certain days designated "alcohol-free." For the first time in the history of the country, Pétain established a minimum drinking age, set at fourteen. In Volnay, where wine was as necessary as oxygen to sustain life, Pétain's betrayal stung. Once, the vintners of the region had gifted Pétain with his own vineyard on a hillside slope overlooking Beaune. Now, old men who had lost their sons went there to open their trousers and piss on Pétain's vines, as unholy an act as could be imagined in Burgundy.

FOR A TIME, GASTON LATOUR GAVE UP his lazy pursuit of
Simone in favour of the relative safety of the vineyard. He
told himself he was biding his time. The land couldn't hold
him. He hated the drudgery of the work, the air thick with
either pollen or dust depending on the season, the dirt under
his fingernails, the strain on his back. Even the strict geometry
of the rows of vines ate away at his nerves. Each plant was an
equal distance from the next, each line relentlessly straight,
with no room for chance or deviation. Every reckless weed that
encroached upon this orderliness was ripped out by its roots.

The old stone farmhouse made Gaston feel claustrophobic
with its brocade couches no one sat on anymore and its dusty
pictures of people lost before he ever knew them. His parents,
frozen in time as bride and groom, were strangers to him, but
relics to Eugénie, a martyr to their memory and to her lost
twin. But if Julien were never to return, what then? People lost
each other all the time, especially during war. People vanished
from each other's lives. There were plenty of vintners in the
area who salivated whenever he mentioned the possibility of
selling the Latour estate. Gaston, a gambler looking for the
easy chance, had plans that didn't include a life of drudgery,
his own sister be damned. She might even marry some village
dullard, if only she'd try.

That summer the only sounds louder than complaints against
the *Service du travail obligatoire* and Pétain were the growling
stomachs of Volnay. The food supply had sunk so low, even in
the countryside, that people ate fox and squirrels. The gravelly
soil so good for the vines was the ruin of many vegetables. A
radish was a luxury. An onion was a meal.

Some of the villagers were so hungry they became obsessed
with food. At night they did not dream of the breasts and thighs
of their lovers, but of the plumpness of a capon. By day, they
tormented themselves with visions of golden croissants, each
flaky layer rich with butter. Any farm animals left uneaten
became, in turn, a challenge to feed, while wild animals that

managed to evade the hunters grew desperate and crept closer to the village. The grocer claimed he'd heard a boar snuffling in his vegetable patch and the next morning found hoof prints where once there had been potatoes. Armand's mother, who kept a goat for its milk, discovered an empty tether one day and a suspicious trail of blood leading away from her house. Madeleine began to worry about the swans.

One Sunday in June, Madeleine waved goodbye to her parents and took her basket out to the forest to search for mushrooms. She didn't go to church anymore. Talk about God made her skin itch and her head dizzy. She knew Armand would be there, kneeling to Our Lady of the Vines in a pool of black cloth. Sometimes she had nightmares in which the black uniform of the priest became indistinguishable from the black uniform of the Gestapo and she would shudder awake, grateful to be delivered from both. She preferred to believe in things that were alive, like birds or true feelings or colours. She thought maybe church was something you should set aside at a certain age like dolls or imaginary playmates. Or maybe she had just taken the wrong path, opened the wrong door, and was now unable to find her way back, too forsaken to look upon Armand's face.

Because Madeleine no longer went to church, she did not hear the terrible news until much later in the day when she returned home. Her mama was prostrate on the couch, fanning herself with her hands, her face as white as ice.

"What is it, Mama? What's happened?"

"The Milice, may they rot in hell, have arrested Léa's father. They say he's been treating men involved with the Resistance. They led him through the village in handcuffs and marched him across the fields to Pommard where they threw him in a cell in the *gendarmerie*. Imagine, the finest man in town—next to your papa, of course—led through the streets like a criminal. Madeleine, you cannot—"

But she was already gone, running as fast as she could, chased by a feeling of dread. She had no plan, no hope, no premonition, only the certainty that she must see for herself what was happening, and that Léa and Dr. Legard needed her.

A small grumbling crowd had gathered at the entrance to the *gendarmerie*. Madeleine scanned the closed faces, skipping over Armand's with a quick breath, but she could not see Léa. She was pushing her way forward through the currents of silent hostility when a scream sliced through the air, the high-pitched wail of a child. She whirled around, following the reverberations of that cry of terror until she came to the mouth of a cul-de-sac.

A little boy in his Sunday-best trembled in a doorway, pinned there by a ferocious white dog with dark scars across his body and face. The child was so frightened he couldn't move. His eyes were screwed tight and his ankle socks and shoes were soaked in a puddle of his own urine.

Madeleine took a step forward and the dog lunged, his teeth sinking into the soft flesh of the boy's thigh, dragging him to the ground. More screams, shouts, pounding footsteps—but Madeleine heard nothing. She walked forward steadily, her open palms outstretched. She saw inside the dog's eyes. She saw that the dog was terrified of stones, knives, thunder, and human beings. She did not pity him, even as she counted his ribs and the scars that told the story of the savagery of his life. *No*, she hummed to him in her soft cadence, *you are brave*, brave enough to have survived the beatings and the perversity of the human race. She put a hand on his muzzle and his mouth opened as if she had sprung a trap. She leaned against him and whispered into his torn ear. *Go. Run.*

But the dog had nowhere to run, except toward the crowd that had gathered at the top of the lane. The bullet hit him square in the chest, dropping him like a stone.

Madeleine staggered back, the last anguished gasp of the dog's breath pulsing through her own body. Then she scooped the fallen child up into her arms and carried him past the stunned villagers straight up to the door of the *gendarmerie*.

"Open up," she commanded and her voice was like thunder. A Milice officer appeared in the doorway, his eyes the colour of gunmetal. He fell back when he saw the child, "What's happened to him?" he cried.

"He needs a doctor," Madeleine replied. "You'd better let Dr. Legard go. Or, you could explain to all these people why you denied medical help to a mere boy."

The crowd surged forward behind Madeleine, backing her up, every eye on the officer, every face threatening. Madeleine noticed Léa then, sitting in the corner, her face ruined by tears. Their eyes met, and Madeleine felt a rush of love from her so pure and so strong she believed she could fly, or maybe even be happy again.

FOR THE SEVENTEEN, NOW EIGHTEEN years of her life, the villagers of Volnay had fed on rumours, speculations, half-truths and certain lies about Madeleine. She was, alternately or simultaneously, a dazzling girl with a lion's heart, a witch, a slut, a wild child, an idiot *savant*, and a cautionary tale.

For her own part, Madeleine was completely unselfconscious. She had never learned the art of looking at herself through other people's eyes. She had no pretences, no artificial poses. She was oblivious to the fact that, in Volnay, she had become theatre, a spectacle to be gazed upon. She might be the classic figure of the holy fool on one day, the debauched star-crossed lover on the next, or the mysterious animal charmer on yet another.

Wherever she walked, she aroused deep emotions, whirlwinds of desire, fear, hope, or joy. The priest and the Germans avoided her, baffled by her fearless unpredictability. Some of the more pious villagers crossed themselves and clucked their tongues as she passed by. Those who had heard the music of her voice swore she cast the spell of a siren and they dreamed at night of watery fates. Others looked upon her luminous face and remembered the thrill of their first kiss, or their first luscious taste of a great wine. She was the village's very own mystery, the bewildering beauty of Volnay.

So it was no surprise that all eyes were upon Madeleine when she went to meet her papa and instead met Simone Benoir leaving the laundry. Simone jumped back a little, as if she had come upon some quick-moving unexpected creature like a bee or a darting squirrel. She wore a pretty dress and raised her chin a little when she noticed Madeleine's drab skirt and her sweater unravelling at the cuffs. She spoke to Madeleine as if in the middle of a conversation that had already begun inside her head.

"It was Gaston, you know."

Madeleine didn't know. She was distracted by the scents of lemon and soap floating in the air. "Pardon?" she managed.

"It was Gaston who shot the dog. The Milice were quite impressed with him. The dog might have gotten away otherwise."

If only, Madeleine thought.

"They say it might have had rabies. Who knows who else it might have attacked."

Madeleine shook her head. "He was not diseased. He would have bitten me if he were. He was just a poor, starving animal. We might have sheltered and fed him instead of shooting him."

"That's absurd. Everyone says you were reckless. That little boy, sweet little Pierre, might have been killed."

"But he wasn't. He wears his bandage like a badge of honour, and I've seen him running and playing in the village."

Simone didn't like to be bested. She leaned toward Madeleine and her words came out with glittery, brittle edges. "Well, Armand Valleray's mother says you are as wild as that dog. She told me so. Her son has saved himself from you. He's returning to Paris in September and he's going to be a priest. You'll have to give him up."

"I already have," Madeleine answered simply.

Simone looked startled and perhaps uneasy. She drew back and gathered her defences around her, her fingers skimming over her shiny hair, her hands smoothing down the pleats in her pretty blue dress. "Gaston is my fiancé now. You probably haven't been paying attention to things like that, but a lot of the young men have left the village. I don't know where the girls from Volnay are going to find husbands. But we're sure to have a splendid party after the wedding. I'll invite you, if you like."

Madeleine heard the words, but was listening more attentively to what lay beneath them. She had an impulse to reach out and touch Simone to stem the flow of insecurity, but there were so many cracks in Simone's surface that Madeleine didn't know where best to place her hands to stop the leaks. She stood still as Simone walked away and felt a little sorry for her for caring so much about Gaston Latour.

That night, however, Simone's words rattled around in her head. It was true that she hadn't been paying attention. Over a meagre supper, she studied her parents. Papa's full head of curly hair was almost white now, giving him the fluffy look of an owl. His shoulders stooped a little when he was especially tired or when the news on the banned radio was especially bad. She realized it had been some time since she had heard him whistle a tune. When her Mama drank wine, her skin flushed rose and she seemed like a girl again. But when she was sad, her skin became a shadowy blue, and there were lines on her face that marked the passing years. There was one line for Madeleine's menagerie, another for her romantic escapade with Armand, two more for her journey into the blackness.

Madeleine gripped the edge of the table, feeling the future rush towards her, unknowable and absolutely unavoidable. It swept through her like an icy blue wind. She staggered to her feet, kissed away the alarm on her parents' faces, and went outside. She climbed into the cherry tree and searched the stars to uncover a clue to her fate. The moon seemed tiny in the vast darkness, a single teardrop in the night sky.

What would become of her? She had been cured of love. No church bells would ring for her as she knelt before an altar in a frothy veil. There would be no children. No baby's heart would beat inside her body, no tiny mouth would search blindly for her breast. Madeleine could feel herself becoming invisible, as translucent as glass. The stars blinked down at her, gave her no answers, and promised nothing.

The very next day, Madeleine sought out Léa and laid her problem at her feet. "What am I to do? I must *do* something."

"With your voice, you could become a *chanteuse*, the queen of Paris."

"Is it that hopeless?"

"No, silly. You could help Eugénie. Gaston's only hiding out at the vineyard to avoid the Germans. Things are going badly for them in Russia. My father says there is a huge army amassing in the south of England preparing for an invasion. The exemption for vineyards will end soon, and Gaston's time so-called helping Eugénie will end with it."

"He's going to marry Simone."

"Is he?"

"You don't believe her? She told me. She even invited me to the wedding party."

"I believe her. I just don't trust Gaston. Do you want me to arrange things with Eugénie?"

"Yes, please Léa."

"And you will be careful? Whenever Gaston is around?"

"Of course."

IT WAS THE BEST JULY MADELEINE COULD REMEMBER. Papa had polished his old bicycle and pumped its tires, and every morning she pedalled through the dew and mist under a pearl-coloured sky to the Latour estate. When it was clear that the dog that had once limped would never leave her, she had given it a name. Achilles now bounded beside her, all four paws in the air with each bound, and ears flying. Colours leapt at her: lime green vines, purple stalks of iris and lupine, orange roses, cloudy bouquets of Queen Anne's lace.

Eugénie was teaching her the names of the birds and each one seemed a small miracle to Madeleine: the turquoise king-fisher, the black-crowned night heron, the turtle doves, the green-bellied bee-eaters, the honey buzzards, and the hoopoe with its flashy orange-and-black crown of feathers.

Best of all, Eugénie led her into the stable where the air was filled with a sweet, green smell and where the old work horse Jacques, with his chocolate hide and flaxen mane, watched Madeleine from the corner of his dark, almost purple eyes, waiting patiently for her attention. When she ran to him, he rubbed his big head against her shoulder and whinnied.

"But there are four stalls here," Madeleine said. Instantly, she wished she hadn't spoken for Eugénie winced.

"Julien rode away on his own horse. The Germans took the others," Eugénie said bitterly.

For a moment, she looked as if she couldn't say more; the memory was too raw. But eventually, she continued, "I saw level-headed men weep when the Germans led away the youngest, strongest horses. And where are they now? Trapped in some airless factory being worked to a slow, painful death, or stiff-limbed and frozen on the Russian front. They only left Jacques because of his swayed back," she sighed.

Then, quickly, she moved away from the pain. "There are bales of straw and hay for Jacques. Are you sure you don't mind? It's hard work."

But Madeleine was lit up with the novelty of being useful. The stable became her special place. She loved the careening, drunken flies, the smell of manure rising, sweet and grassy. She pitched hay and carried cool pails of water from the well. She made beds of straw, bits of it sticking in her hair or drifting up her nose to make her sneeze, and she learned how to groom Jacques with a brush and a curry comb. She led him around the courtyard and up and down the road for exercise, and melted the stiffness of his joints with the warmth of her touch.

She began to share meals with Eugénie, sometimes at the wooden table in the kitchen or, more often, in the vineyard itself, light filtering through the leaves, casting green shadows across their faces. It was an unexpected friendship. Madeleine was air and Eugénie was earth. Madeleine was sky and wind; Eugénie was all about deep roots, the weight of the soil as she held it in her hands, the implacable rhythms of the land. The two women complemented each other and met somewhere in the hazy universe of lost possibilities.

One day, when Eugénie was in the fields, Madeleine went into the house alone and felt its sadness. The rooms smelled like dust, neglect, longing, and bad news. She swept the floors until the bristles of the broom were ragged. She scrubbed the broad pine floorboards until her knees hurt. She blew the dust from the pictures: a bride and groom, innocent of their fate, a soldier—Julien—dark eyes, a square jaw, a steady gaze. When she was finished, surfaces gleamed and light filled the windows.

"Oh," Eugénie whispered when she returned to the house, "I'd forgotten. Please, Madeleine, stay for supper."

They ate a thick bean soup and slices of bread made from milled corn. Eugénie opened a bottle of wine and laughed at Madeleine when she gulped down half a glass, thirsty from all her cleaning.

"You don't know how to drink wine," Eugénie scolded. "It's not like drinking water."

"There's a trick?"

"Not a trick, just a better way of tasting. Hold the wine at the back of your mouth. Let it tell you its story, where it grew, how deep the vines were, what minerals were carried in the grape."

Madeleine smiled. "You're right. It tastes different, better. Did you make this wine?"

"No. We sell our grapes to the larger estates. But some day, well, Julien always dreamed we would have a wine of our very own. There's an old wine press in the stable and a stash of green glass bottles, just in case."

"Tell me about Julien."

Eugénie's mood became pensive. Memories floated in the air, snatches of childhood shared with Julien, games of *cache-cache*, hide-and-seek, picnics in the Morvan forests, wading in streams while silver fish darted between their legs, long sunny days, sudden goodbyes. While Eugénie talked, the light in the windows turned a deep blue and then an inky black. They did not hear Gaston until he was upon them.

"Well, isn't this cosy? Any supper left for me, sister?" His words were flung in Eugénie's direction, but his eyes were set on Madeleine.

Achilles, curled up at Madeleine's feet, canted his head and growled.

"Where have you been?" Eugénie demanded. "You haven't been here for days. Madeleine has worked so hard."

"Ah, yes, the lovely Madeleine."

"Hello Gaston," Madeleine sighed. "It's late. We didn't notice the time. I'll go now."

"Are you forgetting the curfew?"

Madeleine thought that Gaston must have forgotten the curfew, too. Unless he'd been outside for a long time, listening to them, watching them. "I don't pay much attention to the curfew," she said finally.

"So I've heard," Gaston smiled.

"Oh, leave her alone," Eugénie interrupted. "You must stay Madeleine. I'll get you some blankets—you can sleep in Julien's room."

Madeleine followed her friend out of the kitchen, but not before she heard Gaston whisper, "Watch out for ghosts."

Madeleine couldn't sleep. She was alert to every sound, every footstep. Achilles quivered beside her, aware of every taut nerve. She forced herself to relax. At some point, she must have drifted off and was awakened by voices. In the adjacent room, Eugénie and Gaston were arguing. They kept their voices quiet but their exchanges were charged with anger or desperation and neither seemed willing to give in. When it didn't stop, Madeleine got up, went to the window and raised the sash. It was a short drop to the ground. She dressed herself, signalled to Achilles, and together they slipped out into the night.

As she crossed the garden behind the house, she thought she saw a torch light flicker in the room she'd just left, but she couldn't be sure. She leaned into the shadows and was gone.

A WEEK PASSED AND SUMMER DRIFTED into the malaise of August. With the harvest beckoning, the weather was crucial now. The sky was scrutinized for sun, rain, hail, omens of good fortune and portents of doom.

Perhaps another girl might not have returned to the Latour estate. But Madeleine worried that Eugénie had too much to do alone and she missed her. Gaston made her uncomfortable but, in the end, it didn't matter. She was needed and she could only remain true to herself. She knew no other way.

So Madeleine returned to Eugénie's open arms and resumed her routines. She checked and watered the pale pink roses planted at the end of every row of vines. If they were healthy, the vines would be healthy too. She combed Jacques' mane and tail and made his old coat shine. She picked the bushes thickening with *myrtilles* and made jam with a bit of amber honey that Eugénie had traded for wine. With luck, the jam would last the winter.

But the inevitable was waiting. Gaston had watched Madeleine for too long. He could not keep watching her and do nothing. He found her in the stable.

"We're alone," he said. "Eugénie has gone into the village. I watched her leave."

Madeleine stood very still. She noticed how his eyes darted from her to the gaping door of the stable and back to her. At her feet, Achilles growled. She heard the heavy thud of Jacques' hoof against the stable door.

Gaston took a step forward.

She took a step back.

His figure was backlit by the sun. For an instant, Madeleine saw him shrouded in a black mist, nothing she could touch or hold. The mist smelled like cinders and soot, the ashes of desire and dashed hopes. The mist floated towards her, stinging her eyes until she could barely see.

He was close now. His touch was hot. It spread along her body like a painful rash and she flinched from him.

He slapped her hard across the cheek, cracking her neck. As she fell, she heard frenzied kicking from Jacques' stall, saw Gaston's boot swinging towards her, Achilles' desperate leap, a yelp of pain ripping through the air as Gaston's boot connected with the body of the small dog.

She staggered to her feet, rage flooding through her like an undammed river, loosing her screams, pumping strength into her hands and arms as she grasped the currycomb and raked it across his face.

Blood leapt to the surface of his skin in ragged lines. He stopped, stunned, saw the red on his fingers and then lunged for her, thrusting one hand between her legs, the other clamping her breast.

Madeleine twisted away, crashing into the barrel of wine bottles, an explosion of glass. And then: her hands searching blindly for a weapon, her hands gripping the neck of a bottle, swinging the bottle with her full body weight.

She felt a terrible jolt along the length of her arm. Pure red flared behind her eyes.

When she could see again, Gaston lay still on the floor of the stable. There was a moment of profound silence as if the world had stopped breathing.

Madeleine crawled over to Achilles and gathered him into her arms. A patch of blood marked where his head had crashed against a stall door, and the fur behind his right ear oozed. He licked her hand once as she rocked him, stroking his forehead and murmuring words of comfort until finally, with a single rattle, the small body went limp, the light in his eyes snuffed out by death. She kissed him and gently closed his eyes.

She forced herself to look at Gaston. Shards from the bottle were caught in his hair where they shone like spears of icy grass in a thin trail of blood.

And then she couldn't stand to look any more. She ran and ran, ran like the white dog with the black scars, ran like the wolves that howled through the nightmares of Burgundy, ran until she collapsed across Léa's threshold.

She opened her mouth to say the awful thing that she had done, but she could not. Her mouth opened and closed on no sound.

SIMONE

SIMONE BENOIR SMILED AT HERSELF in the mirror and began to brush her chestnut hair. Her whole life was about to change and you couldn't even tell by looking at her. She could almost forget who she was before and what had happened to her.

She leaned forward, closer to her reflection. Pretty, but not beautiful, she decided. Her dark eyes were lovely, but her chin was a little pointed, her nose a little flat. She knew her face well, knew how it could flush with desire, how her eyes could widen in mock surprise, how an inscrutable smile could hide a secret. Yet, no matter how often she looked, her mirror still seemed to reflect the face of a stranger, the face of the new Simone, the one she'd invented for Volnay. In fact, Simone had told so many lies, to so many people for so long, it was impossible to know which parts of her, if any, were real.

For many months, Simone had tried not to wonder what would happen next. Her parents thought this was the best way to survive the war—just live in the here and now, one day at a time, without the tortuous doubts and long shadows cast by an uncertain future. But Simone saw this could easily be just another way to lie to herself, the way she had lied in Paris. The future was a treacherous, unpredictable thing. You had to catch it out, or it would slip away from you completely, like a feral cat slinking into the dark night.

It went without saying that Simone's parents, when they did speak to each other, did not speak of the past. Whenever it was accidentally alluded to, her mother would snatch up a lace handkerchief and press it against her temples.

Simone did not wish to leave Paris, but she recognized a good idea when it was forced upon her. Her father, a successful *négociant* in the family tradition, had visited Burgundy dozens and dozens of times: a hospitable, charming place, he'd promised, full of gentle landscapes and refined cuisine, all that was necessary for *l'art de vivre*. Simone had imagined the colour burgundy, a deep red, almost purple shade, suggestive of power and opulence. So she had willingly helped her parents pack up the contents of their beautiful apartment on the rue de Passy in the 16th Arrondissement of Paris, carefully wrapping the crystal in swaths of tissue paper, draping the delicate furniture under yards of white muslin, and shipping the family portraits off to the Bank of France for safe-keeping, as if the whole family, even its ghosts, were going on a long holiday.

When Simone first looked upon Volnay, buried among the dips and rises of the region's chalky hills, she felt she had been hit with a stone between her eyes. It was nothing more than a few dozen houses huddled around an incongruous pond and an obligatory church.

"This is it? This is where you've brought us?" Simone glared at her father.

"To live well, my dear, it is best to live hidden."

"Buried is more like it."

"Nonsense. It's an easy walk to Pommard. You can accompany me on business trips to Beaune and to Dijon anytime you like. The country air will do you good."

Simone stared at her father until he was forced to dip his head and look away. At that instant, she knew she'd been tricked. She remembered the endless talks at breakfasts about putting sand bags in the Louvre and putty around the stained glass in Notre Dame as protection against German shelling. A trail of newspapers had been left deliberately in her way so that she could not avoid the threatening headlines. She'd gone to

Sunday lunches with the whole Benoir clan only to hear their grumbling about that bully Haussmann who, a hundred years earlier, had stretched, widened, and wrenched the winding lanes and alleys of old Paris, and made a city of wide boulevards spacious enough for German tanks.

It was all a ruse, all that spooky talk about the war. The point was not that the Germans would march into Paris—that was inevitable—but that Simone would be marched out, trapped in the countryside under the loving thumb of her father. She had to admit that he'd played his hand well. It served her well and truly right.

The house they settled into was comfortable, at least. It had a massive fireplace in the living room and French windows that opened onto a shady, cobblestoned courtyard. It was, by far, the grandest house in the vicinity of Volnay.

They brought no servants, of course. Young girls did not aspire to be maids any longer and the chauffeur had run off to join the army. Simone's mother, however, had no ambition to be anything other than rich and she had learned to do nothing other than to draw adequately and play the piano poorly. So, it was a great relief that Augustine, the cook, wanted to leave Paris too, brought up as she'd been with barbarous stories of the Hun raping women and children and grinding their bones for bread.

She had a young nephew, Pierre, very sweet and obedient, whose parents were poor: would Monsieur Benoir allow him to come, too? He would, much to Simone's disappointment, for she'd once caught Pierre snooping in her bedroom in Paris, and thought him a two-faced brat.

The country house in Volnay had windows facing in every direction. "How glorious," Simone's father said. "We shall be bathed in light."

But it was the wrong light, not at all the soft rose of Paris. The light in Burgundy was often hazy in the mornings, sifting across the vines like gossamer and blurring edges. At midday, it could be harsh, spilling into the gaps between puffy clouds, and etching deep shadows. In Simone's eyes, the whole countryside was garishly sunny and blooming.

She longed for a building tall enough to interrupt the undulating horizon. When she stood for a long time at her window, the rows upon rows of geometric lines formed by the vines made her feel sick and dizzy. Everywhere she looked she saw green. Her eyes were so bombarded with every shade of green imaginable that even her dreams were tinted green. She swore she would never again wear that colour and tossed out every sweater, skirt, dress, sock, and ribbon cursed with that pervasive shade. When the Germans finally did come, Simone felt it a bitter irony that their uniforms were a peculiar shade of grey-green.

FOR A VERY LONG TIME, or at least what seemed like a long time to her, Simone behaved. She spent as little time as possible in Volnay, preferring instead the company of her cousins who had settled in Beaune. She often accompanied her father on trips to Dijon, but even the glorious palace of the once powerful Dukes of Burgundy seemed puny in her eyes compared to the effortless grace of Paris.

Eventually, though, even these small pleasures disappeared. By 1942, travel restrictions had grown cumbersome. Cars, even her father's, disappeared. Trains were crowded with sweaty, grumbling people, scouring the countryside for food. Celebrations, even around Bastille Day, dried up. Gaiety evaporated.

As an only and spoiled child, Simone wasn't used to the sidelines, but she was forced to stand on them more or less impatiently now, and she resigned herself to learning the ways of the village.

Her first classroom was the church, filled with godliness and gossip. In Paris, she and her parents were often careless about the Lord's Day, choosing picnics in the Bois de Boulogne over prayers if the weather was fine. But missing church in Volnay was unthinkable. The square stone building squatted like a toad behind the village's memorial to a generation of young men lost in the Great War. Every expense on the church had apparently been spared.

Inside the heavy wooden doors, Simone counted three flanking chapels on either side of the nave, each with a small painting executed by amateurs in mostly muddy colours; one confessional booth with a flimsy red velvet curtain that she guessed would not muffle many secrets; and one plaster Virgin with a cracked nose, surrounded by dripping prayer candles. When Simone complained about the starkness of the church, she was directed by her mother to look upon the glory of Our Lady of the Vines, the white stone carving of the Virgin and Child which stood behind the church and high among the trees, looking down benevolently on the hillsides of vines below. Simone searched her mother's face for any sign of irony, but found none.

The villagers themselves seemed to stand, sit, sing, and kneel as one. Many of the men, she knew, were friends or business acquaintances of her father. Most looked bent over and leather-skinned—they were, after all, farmers, even though they thought of themselves as artists or craftsmen, masters of the mystery of wine making. The women wore better clothes and had straighter backs. They carried themselves with dignity and still wore hats and gloves to church to show their good manners. The old women wore black from head to toe, widows or sonless mothers, casualties of the last ravaging war.

Simone had to look hard to find the fraying edges. The German soldiers who guarded the village, and more specifically, the villagers' wine, prayed alone at the back of the church. No one would sit with them. They had stolen too much—food, horses, pride. The villagers resented the fact that they prayed to the same god, and were fond of saying that the Germans would probably steal Christ too, if they thought they could get him on a train.

Simone picked out Gaston Latour on one rainy Sunday, sprawled in his pew, long legs jutting into the aisle, an exquisitely bored, handsome face under a shock of black hair. She learned his name and that of his sister from her father. Simone determined to make friends with Eugénie who bowed her head piously in church and seemed always to be praying furiously for something or someone.

The most popular girl was Léa, the doctor's daughter, tall and rangy and spirited, always surrounded by people at the end of the service eager for a share of her smile. She was often trailed by a slim girl with hair the colour of marigolds in the sun. Simone gave the girl little attention, for her face was often blank, emptied of all content, like the chalk circle of a child's drawing.

But all of that changed one dreary Sunday in 1942. From out of the belly of the gloomy church, a bird rose above the drone of the priest's voice. A dove fluttered frantically along the shadowy chapel walls, its wings a blur as it swooped down the transept, carving a path blindly above the heads of the congregation. The girl with the marigold hair stretched her hand into the air and the dove settled into her palm the way a tired head might sink into a pillow. Suddenly, the girl's face shone with a radiance that lit up the whole church. She was so beautiful that Simone caught her breath.

"Who is that?" she whispered.

And the whole congregation seemed to whisper back as one. "Madeleine. Madeleine Vernoux."

IN PARIS, SIMONE HAD SUFFERED all the symptoms of love: dizziness and desire, staring at the night sky for portents, a lurching in the pit of her stomach, and real hunger, just to see her lover, as if this would ever be enough. The cure, apparently, was to be buried in Volnay, where no one talked about desire and the word *sex* was never spoken aloud.

But perhaps her judgment was flawed, for over the next

several weeks, the villagers clucked and whispered and wondered and buzzed until their collective voices swept like a worrisome wind throughout Volnay, alarmed by the indiscreet and indelicate courtship of Madeleine Vernoux and Armand Valleray.

It was all nonsense to Simone. Fallen women were common: all you had to do to qualify was lift up your skirt before marriage. You would think that the last war, with all its fallen young men, would have convinced people to judge less harshly. Better to live in the moment, love in the moment, before the young men vanished.

Simone had seen the lovers herself as she gazed wistfully through her bedroom window—the dark head and the golden head, each leaning toward the other, arms encircling waists, as they strode up the sloping hills towards the protective screen of the forest, oblivious to the villagers who were left behind to imagine all sorts of mischief under the trees. She could not decide whether the marigold girl was incredibly brave or incredibly stupid. She bore her no ill will, but she knew that no love affair could stay shiny and new forever.

Simone herself had been schooled in the politics of love, the pretty words and poses, the manipulative tears, the terrible cunning beneath the skin. She was, alas, her mother's daughter and she had watched her mother spurn and coddle and infuriate her father all her young life.

When Madame Benoir wanted something, her voice became light and airy—she would mention the dress, the painting, the piece of furniture, the opera tickets, ever so carelessly, as if the wanted object was nothing at all that mattered to her. That was when Simone had learned to be especially wary, for if her father said no, no one was safe. One day she would be the perfect daughter, and the next she would be slapped for spilling juice on the tablecloth. She would climb onto her mother's lap one day and be roughly pushed away the next. Her mother's love was like the sun on a bright, cold winter's day. It didn't warm her, but it reminded her of warmth and left her hungering for it.

She once dreamed of love the way little girls do, the kind of glamorous passion seen in the flickering images of the cinema screen—the lights go down, and the violins surge, and even the most ordinary gestures become extraordinary. Everything stops and something you can't explain begins.

But Simone now knew that wasn't true. Love was schemes and tricks, hot words spit into the air that burned the skin when they landed. It was her father pacing up and down, shouting and slamming his fist into walls. It was her mother's tears and tantrums, the way she could turn a cheek to you, so cold your lips would freeze as they grazed her skin.

On the bad days, she would run to Augustine for comfort. Unlike her stylish and skittish mother, Augustine was round and soft with arms that were always opened wide.

"Don't worry, little one," she would say. "The storm is almost over. I happen to know that your papa has already ordered that painting and when it arrives, it'll be summer again."

And soon after that, Simone thought but never said, winter again. Her mother never knew how much was enough. She seemed to always be looking for that someplace or that something that would give her some other life worth living, leaving Simone alone and haunted by a sense that she had failed in some fundamental, but indefinable way.

Simone remembered the day little Pierre was in the kitchen talking to his aunt during one of the maternal storms.

"What do you think of my mother?" she'd asked. She'd expected him to be a little frightened of Madame Benoir—at the very least to be on Simone's side.

The seven-year-old boy flicked a glance at his aunt to see if Simone really wanted him to tell the truth. Augustine nodded, and Pierre had looked Simone in the eye as he spoke. "Your mama always smells nice, like she costs a lot of money."

Simone laughed, but she knew the little boy had told a bigger truth than he knew. Everything about her mother came from a bottle: delicate perfumes and skin creams, herbal cures for headaches, opiates for soothing nerves, and, of course, wine, the source of her husband's fortune. She wondered how it would be to have a mother, really. Someone who looked at you approvingly, at least once, every day.

THE VILLAGE CAME DOWN HARD on Madeleine and Armand. When it became clear that the outrageous marriage would not be allowed and that, shortly after, Armand had disappeared, Simone went to visit Armand's mother under the guise of consoling her. She hoped to discover what had become of her son.

Madame Valleray lived in a humble house on one of the muddy lanes of the village. Her hands were cracked from working in Monsieur Vernoux's laundry, just as her heart was cracked from the loss of her husband and the scandal swirling around her son.

Simone poured the tea and made soothing sounds and pretended to care, while Madame Valleray poured out her disappointment. "She's a wild thing, that girl. Undisciplined. Monsieur Vernoux is a kind man, but he and his wife have always doted on her too much. They say she climbs into a tree in her back yard on moonlit nights, with the wind rushing past her, crazy as a bat. She cast a spell over my boy, that's the truth."

Simone was intrigued. Madeleine sounded like the most interesting person yet in Volnay. *Maybe if I had climbed into a goddamned tree*, Simone thought, *Papa would have let me stay in Paris.*

"But where has your boy gone?" she prodded. "Surely he wouldn't abandon you?"

"Oh, no. He's a good boy. I brought him up good and proper."

"Yes, but where has he gone?"

But Madame Valleray clamped her thin lips shut and Simone could not cajole her into saying another word.

As time passed, and still Armand did not return, she took to studying Madeleine whenever she saw her in the marketplace. People nudged each other as Madeleine passed by. Some of the villagers looked at her with a mournful tenderness, seeming to empathize with her disgrace and her pain. Others avoided her and even seemed frightened of her, but whether sympathizers or judges, no one spoke to her. She was the scarecrow in the garden.

SIMONE WAS ESPECIALLY BORED on the day her mother took her along to the confessional. She hadn't planned to lie or be blasphemous. It's just that the priest was so officious and her mother was trying to look so pious. Simone knelt, crossed herself, and cleared her throat. "Bless me, Father, for I have sinned."

Simone saw the profile of the priest settle in behind the grille, nose seeming to sniff the air for sin. There were moth holes in the red velvet curtain and Simone could see that her mother was in a perfect position to overhear everything. Her parenting consisted of praying for Simone and fearing her perdition. She gave lessons in morality, and an austere and depressing morality at that. These were standards, of course, from which she was personally exempt.

"Tell me, child. Open your heart to the Lord," the priest urged.

"Well, Father, there has been the usual cursing, and not enough honouring of my parents who have brought me to this wretched village. In the past two weeks, I've slept with, let me count—twelve boys. Oh, and two of their fathers."

The priest was still sputtering, his face having flushed an alarming shade of red, when Madame Benoir ripped back the curtain, yanked her daughter by the arm, and frog-marched her home.

There ensued twenty minutes of Madame Benoir's hysteria—arm-flinging, china-smashing, and finally door-slamming hysteria, as Simone and her father gazed on.

Left alone after the fury had departed, Monsieur Benoir pulled at his beard and regarded his daughter with piercing eyes, unblinking, behind round glasses with steely wired frames. "Why do you do these things, Simone?"

"I'm sorry, Papa."

"No, I don't believe you are. Not one bit. That poor priest—are there twelve young men in Volnay?"

"I don't know. I hope so."

"Simone."

"Sorry, Papa. Mother began talking to me about learning to do something useful. She mentioned flower arranging and playing the harp."

"Really? What's useful about flower arranging?"

"She was rambling on about planting vegetables and knitting circles. I was desperate to distract her."

"Perhaps you could find a more suitable way, something short of an emotional ambush. After all, she still hasn't fully recovered from—"

Simone was quite used to hearing sentences remain suspended whenever the topic of conversation returned to her escapades in Paris.

Monsieur Benoir pushed aside the awkwardness with another question. "Would a knitting circle be so bad? You might meet some other nice young ladies."

Simone looked at him incredulously.

"You have to *try*, Daughter. I know you're lonely. In Paris, you were sought after, asked everywhere. Too much there, too little here, I know. But you're young. You'll mend, and the war and your exile will not last forever."

Simone kept her head down. She would not let him see the tears stinging her eyes.

"You know I must punish you?"

"Yes, Papa."

"Very well. Go to your room—Augustine will bring a light meal on a tray. Stay out of your mother's way and the dining

room for a couple of days. And tomorrow, you must visit the
priest and apologize."

Simone nodded and left the drawing room quickly. As she
pulled open the door, she caught Pierre eavesdropping. He
stuck his tongue out at her and scampered away.

In Paris, Simone's bedroom had told a story—a spill of ce-
lebrity and fashion magazines across a bedside table; a pretty
little dressing-table trimmed in gold with curved legs, its surface dusted with talc and face powder; an oval mirror with
invitations and advertisements for various jazz clubs tucked
into its frame. Her room in Paris looked like someone could
be happy in it.

Here, it felt like she was being shut up in a cell. All the party
dresses had been left behind with the parties. Her plain, pine
dressing-table held a brush and comb set, and one smuggled
tube of lipstick that she hardly bothered to wear anymore.
Her walls were bare, but for the strategically placed crucifix
above her bed. Simone was staring at it, her thoughts far from
the suffering of Jesus, when she heard a quick, sharp tap on
the window.

A bird, she thought, if she thought at all. A volley of raps
brought her to her feet. Hailstones, perhaps? The whole of
Volnay would be mobilized for hailstones, though little could
be done to save the vines if the storm were fierce enough.

She opened the French windows that looked down upon
the courtyard and stared at the sky. The clouds were moving
quickly, sweeping past the moon, and anyone who had any
sense was surely fast asleep.

"Down here," the voice called, at first startling her into taking
a step back. But her curiosity pulled her forward and she peered
into the courtyard, her eyes slowly adjusting to the darkness.

It was Gaston Latour, leaning against the courtyard wall.
He looked dishevelled—for he must have scaled the walls to
get into the courtyard. Wild licks of dark hair fell across his
forehead. "Are you coming or not?" he challenged.

Simone was not even conscious of making a decision. She simply slipped on an extra sweater and tiptoed down the stairs.

Just as she reached the kitchen door, Pierre spoke. "Where are you going?"

"Damn, Pierre, you scared me. What are you doing up at this hour?"

Little Pierre stood his ground. "Where are you going?"

"Listen, Pierre. This is important. We're friends, right?"

The child said nothing, but nodded tentatively.

"You know what a promise is?"

Another nod.

"A promise is a secret that you keep, that you don't tell anybody, ever. You understand that?"

"Ever and ever?"

"Not even Aunt Augustine. If you ever tell, something bad will happen to me."

"Will you be put in jail?"

"What? Why would you think that?"

"Auntie said you might have been put in jail if you hadn't left Paris."

"Nonsense. Papa would never let that happen. So will you promise to keep our secret? I'll give you a franc."

"Five francs. That way I'll be sure not to tell."

"Fine, little beast. Now go to bed."

Simone stepped out into the night.

"Over here," Gaston whispered. He was kneeling by the arched gate now, busy unlatching it.

"What are you doing?"

"Leaving the gate open, unless you want to climb the walls to get back in."

"Who says I'm going anywhere?"

"Do you have other plans?"

"I—no."

"Then follow me. Keep low, and no talking until we get to the chapel."

"What chapel?"

Gaston put a finger to his lips and opened the gate.

Darkness seemed to rush through the archway, and Simone hesitated. Gaston was already disappearing, his shape dissolving into the deep shadows. All at once she felt the urge to move like an itching in her legs. She ran to keep up, down the long lane that led away from her house, across a thin road and into the fields thick with vines, running between rows of vines, feeling childlike and giddy with freedom, invisible in the darkness, her heart beating fast.

She almost slammed into the stone wall marking a *domaine* at the bottom of the sloping vineyard. She could hear Gaston smothering a laugh. "Now what?" she mimed.

In one quick motion, he moved behind her, put his arms around her waist and boosted her up. Her hands found the top of the wall and she vaulted herself up and over, dropping easily onto the grassy verge below. Just beyond was a larger road, and just on the other side of the road, glimmering in the moonlight, a small white chapel.

She was already moving towards it, when Gaston grabbed her by the shoulders and pushed her to the ground.

"German patrol," he whispered. "Stay down."

Face down in the grass, dirt up her nose, and the unidentifiable rustlings of unknown insects all around her, Simone swore never again to live in the countryside of her own volition, should she live through the night. She listened to the hum of an engine in the distance, moving closer, closer, deepening into a metallic whine as it swept past, then fading gradually.

Then she was up and running again across the dirt road, then along the side of the chapel, though a gate, and straight into a graveyard.

She stood still, not moving a muscle, suddenly feeling the chill of the breeze. It felt surreal to be here, like an overly vivid and slightly alarming dream. She wasn't a little girl afraid of ghosts, but there was something unsettling about a graveyard at night, something powerfully sad, smelling of neglect and the sting of loss, something gone forever. The gravestones were old, some of them tilting forwards or sideways. It was too dark to read any of the names or inscriptions, but she knew the words would be there: *Gone too soon, Dearest, Beloved.*

Then she thought about what was gone from her own life and shrugged off the temptation to feel sorry. Surely some of the bodies buried here deserved to be in the ground, and some of the people who put them here were glad to be rid of them, though none had been brave enough to carve their relief into stone. *Good Riddance*, maybe, or *Free at Last.*

"Andres," she whispered, almost involuntarily, surprised that the name still hurt when she spoke it aloud. She should despise him. She almost did.

"Who's Andres?" Gaston asked.

"Nothing. Nobody. Why are we here?"

"C'mon. I've something to show you. Our vineyard is just there on the far side of the chapel."

Simone followed him to a tiny hut in the middle of his vineyard. Many of the *domaines* used the huts to store tools and, now, as her father had told her, to hide secret caches of wine from the Germans. Gaston led her inside, shifted a cask, and pulled open a trapdoor set into the floor.

"You have a cellar here?" Simone exclaimed.

"Well, not a traditional wine cellar—that's next to the house, but this one has treasures of its own."

Simone was expecting a damp, unpleasant space, filled with spiders and dust mites that always made her sneeze. Instead, as Gaston swept a torch round the vaulted ceiling, she saw patterns of brick in pale, russet stone. There were wine racks, boxes and baskets, and wooden containers tidily stacked. The cellar was surprisingly warm, despite the fact that it was underground, like a Métro station on a cold Paris night. The air was dry and slightly scented—an almost spicy scent that Simone couldn't quite name.

Gaston took a bottle from one of the racks and poured her a glass of wine—a cup of wine, actually. There was no fine crystal here. They sat side by side on top of two cartons and toasted each other.

"Thanks for my first night out in Volnay," Simone said.

"My pleasure. I thought you were looking especially bored in church."

She had to laugh at that. If he only knew what she'd done to that stuffy priest. "But how did you find me or even learn my name?"

"Seriously? In Volnay? I could probably tell you what you ate for breakfast. Tell me about Paris."

"No one can tell you about Paris."

"Why not?"

"Because everyone discovers their own Paris. It's different for everyone. It depends on what history you know, what dreams you bring along, what café you visit, which bridges you cross, whatever little shop you run inside when it rains."

"Tell me about your Paris, then."

"My Paris is the loveliest apartment you've ever seen, with windows that overlook the Bois de Boulogne. And there's so much to look at—people and clothes and paintings and cabarets and swing-jazz clubs and..." Simone stopped talking and gulped her wine.

"So why did your family leave?"

"Ever hear of the German army?"

"But the Benoirs are rich, and the rich live in a different territory where they can take good care of themselves."

"Well, that territory, like the past, has borders now. No trespassing allowed."

"Suit yourself, but be careful."

"Careful of what?"

"Volnay loves a good mystery and gossip is a boat full of holes."

"I've nothing to hide."

"Oh yes, you do, Simone. We all have something to hide. Would you like to see what I have hidden?"

He began lifting the lids of the cartons in the cellar, while Simone stared in amazement. There were whole bags of flour, sugar, and coffee, whole wheels of cheese, sacks of potatoes, and cartons of eggs. Gaston looked immensely pleased with himself.

"But where did you get all of this?" Simone asked, finally identifying the spicy aroma in the air as coffee, something she hadn't smelled for a long time.

"We raid the railway yards near Beaune, the trains loaded with French goods heading for Germany."

"You stole this from the Germans?"

"It's not stealing. It's ours to begin with. We're just taking back what's ours."

Simone smiled at the thought of that. She knew a clever lie when she heard it. Gaston wasn't planning to distribute what had once belonged to the villagers of the region. He was planning to sell it back to them on the black market. The villagers would be twice robbed.

She wondered why he was revealing his secret to her, but only briefly. The Benoirs were rich, he'd said so himself. She was there as a likely client.

Well, she thought, at least he is a handsome thief. And there in the cellar, smelling of coffee and sugar, Gaston kissed her and she kissed him back. She'd learned that a kiss meant nothing.

IN THE NEXT FEW DAYS, Simone paid attention to the subtexts of the village in a way she had not bothered about before. She wanted to find out all she could about Gaston. Since their escapade in the night, he'd treated her with a cocky lack of interest whenever they met in the village. But she knew all the games of flirtation. Dissimulation was her natural style, her childhood training at her mother's knee.

She started at breakfast with her father. "So, Papa, tell me about the Latours."

He lowered his newspaper and scratched his beard. He was, first and foremost, a wine merchant, a *négociant*, and it was his business to know all the vineyards of Burgundy. "Their estate is fairly small, on the slopes at the bottom of the village, lower slopes so not likely to produce a *grand cru*."

"I was hoping you'd tell me about the people, not the grapes."

"Oh. Well, I know the parents are both dead, some tragic illness or other. The estate belongs to the three children now. The eldest brother is a POW, god knows where, so Eugénie and Gaston are left to carry on. It's a shame, but as the war goes on, the chances of their saving the vineyard become slimmer."

"Why?"

"Poor harvests, not just at the Latour place, but all over Burgundy. That and terrible shortages. Eugénie is dedicated, but Gaston seems restless. Under normal circumstances, he'd be the younger brother content to be bought out and free to seek his fortune elsewhere. Why are you asking about the Latours suddenly?"

"I'd like to make friends with Eugénie," Simone lied smoothly.

"Now, that's the spirit. Find some young people and start to become part of the village."

"And I'd also like to know where we got these eggs we're eating." She looked around the table—"and this butter, and the flour for the bread."

"Simone!"

"Oh, don't look so surprised, Papa. I know all about Gaston and the black market. Shouldn't you stop him? Isn't it dangerous? What if a German soldier were to see what's on our table? You do business with the Germans."

Her father rose to his feet. She had never seen him so angry, not even after one of her mother's tantrums.

"I don't do business with the Germans. I broker the best price I can, laughable as it is, for the vintners, only because they trust me. No German will ever set foot in this house if I can help it. Whatever Gaston Latour does is his own business and whatever you know or think you know, you'll keep your clever mouth shut. Grow up, Simone. Underneath this veil of normalcy, there's real danger, palpable danger. We are a defeated people, slowly starving in an occupied country. A careless word could get a man shot."

"But what am I supposed to think?" Simone insisted, pointing again to the table.

"You're supposed to think better of me."

He threw down his newspaper in disgust and left the room.

Simone gazed after him and wished she could stroke his beard and kiss his forehead and explain that she hadn't, until that moment, understood the quicksand he navigated as liaison between the Germans and the great wine houses of Burgundy. One step in either direction could make him a resister or a collaborator. And she also understood that being very rich made her father very vulnerable.

SIMONE'S CHANCE TO GROW CLOSER to Eugénie Latour came sooner than she might have hoped. Léa invited both young women to a picnic, an excuse really, something to cheer up Madeleine, who was apparently still pining for her vanished lover. Under normal circumstances, Paris being normal, Simone would have declined. As a little girl she was dragged to visit her stiff and over-perfumed grandmother for afternoon picnics, only to be told she wasn't allowed to speak, fidget, drink the wine, or touch anything. She couldn't imagine a duller way to cheer a friend. Still, she put on a pretty summer dress and looked forward to the event, sweet-talking Gaston into giving her a wedge of contraband cheese to surprise everyone.

They met in the back lawn of the doctor's house. Léa had set a table under the cherry trees and Simone presented her gift of *chambertine* with a flourish.

There was a moment of awkward silence, not the reaction Simone was expecting. Léa's pleasure was immediately overshadowed by suspicion as to the origins of the gift. Eugénie raised her eyebrows at Simone and then looked away quickly, enough of a signal for Simone to understand that she knew the origins of the cheese, and quite a lot about her younger brother, enough to make Simone blush.

Madeleine seemed not to notice at all. She sat on a blanket with a book of poetry on her lap, so still, so inviolate, she looked like a woman caught on canvas by an artist's brush. She was intoxicatingly beautiful and, at the same time, dangerous, with jarring hidden depths. Colours seemed to intensify around her, noises to hush. Simone felt awkward in her presence, clumsy, as if she might blurt out an inappropriate remark or spill something on her dress.

Eugénie, she realized, was asking her about Paris, and Simone wanted to shout out how much better it was than Volnay, how the city hummed with bright possibilities, but all she could think of were her failures there and the words died on her lips. She found herself wishing she could do better, be better. She wished she could undo the past. She even wished that the bright hopes of her girlhood had not been ruined. But, for the first time, she didn't lie to herself—she'd ruined them all by herself.

She replied something or other to Eugénie's question and looked resentfully at Madeleine. Sometimes the marigold girl looked right through you, as if you were a window and something beyond had drawn her attention. Other times, she stared. She was staring at Simone now, memorizing her, drinking in all she had to offer or hide. Simone felt herself unravelling, her facades melting. Instinctively, she crossed her arms over her breast, as if she were naked among strangers. Her heart was beating fast.

Mercifully, Léa's voice broke the spell. "Eugénie, have you had a letter from Julien?"

Simone bowed her head and breathed in deeply. She drank

her wine quickly and held up her glass for more. She listened closely to Eugénie and did not look at Madeleine again.

Julien Latour was in an officer's prisoner of war camp in Silesia. Under the terms of the Geneva Convention, officers were exempt from hard labour and could correspond with their families. But in between the phrases blacked out by the censors, Eugénie had read of the grimness of the camp.

"He loves the land," Eugénie was saying. "He would go rambling for hours, or ride to the Morvan. I keep hearing the gates of the camp shut on his freedom."

Madeleine was genuinely moved. "Oh, how terrible."

The urgency in her voice made it seem like Julien had been captured that very morning, a mere breath away. She talked about him losing his freedom, being locked up, and in the pauses between words, Simone could think of nothing but birds caught in nets, rabbits caught in traps. It made her shiver, as if the summer breeze had turned into a cold Silesian wind.

When the picnic ended, Simone was exhausted and completely deflated. She'd learned nothing about Gaston, except perhaps that he would never match the beloved Julien, made perfect by his misfortune and his absence. And she'd learned far more about Madeleine than she ever cared to know. As far as she was concerned, the girl was crazy dangerous. You couldn't hide a thing from her.

THROUGHOUT THE SUMMER OF 1942, Simone was far from passive, rather she seemed to be constantly pushing against things: doors, limits, rules, propriety, even the Germans. Her tantrums equalled those of her mother, and Pierre would cover his ears to muffle their screaming, running to Augustine for comfort. Simone began to read to him at bedtime, an act mistaken for kindness, committed instead to cloak her deceit. Pierre's room was on the ground floor, making it easier for her to sneak out and meet Gaston. She paid the little boy a small fortune in bribes.

Sometimes, she and Gaston would run to the chapel and tell stories to one another. She never told him the truth and suspected that he didn't either. But she knew that he was lonely like her, though it was a different kind of loneliness.

"Who is Andres?" he asked again and again.

A dream, a memory, a lie, a lullaby, a ghost. The villain in a black cape in a Christmas pantomime.

Simone never told her story to anyone, partly because she was ashamed, partly because she couldn't get past it. She didn't know what she'd find on the other side if she did tell it. Who would she be if she revealed the deepest part of herself? What would be left after the telling? Even her father didn't know the whole story. He only knew fragments, mostly of the end of the story. Only she knew how all the bits fit together, all the dark shards and sharp corners.

Finally, she told Gaston that Andres was a beggar in Paris who lived in the Bois de Boulogne and fed bits of bread to the pigeons. Only when the birds landed on his shoulders and his head would he smile. When he died, all of the birds flew away and never returned to that spot again. It was something of the truth. Enough.

Gaston just laughed. "Fine," he said. "Don't tell me."

She learned he couldn't remember his parents. His mother was a pair of soft hands, a song at bedtime, a scent of lavender. His father was a silhouette in the bedroom doorway, a rolling laugh that filled up all the corners of a room, two strong arms that could swing you into the sky.

She learned that with Eugénie and Julien, he was always outside the circle, on the fringe, an after thought. Gaston saw himself as a loveless boy, orphaned by his parents and peripheral to the emotional ties between Eugénie and Julien. While a lack of love might make some people insecure or reclusive, it had made Gaston greedy, greedy for attention and greedy for adventure. It had made him reckless and, sometimes, a little cruel. Simone did not pity him. He scorned the village and laughed at the dullness of people who only wanted to live calmly and make good wine and die and go to heaven in their due time. He taunted Eugénie because she was not as pretty as her friends; a spinster, he called her, at twenty-three.

One foolhardy night, Simone lay face down with Gaston in the bed of a farm truck driven by Henri, who sold vegetables in the market. They drove all the way without lights to the rail yards just outside of Beaune to raid the trains.

As they jumped down from the truck, Gaston gripped her arm. "If we run into any trouble, you're on your own, understand? You're old enough to answer for yourself if you're caught and the Germans will go easier on a girl."

Simone had no time to ponder this piece of gallantry. She had to run full out to keep up. In the train yard, the huge wheeled and geared machines were like sleeping skeletons of iron dinosaurs in the inky darkness.

"Down here," Gaston called, just out of sight.

She looked for him between trains, down what seemed an endless valley of metal before she spotted him in the shadows.

While she watched, Henri used a crowbar to wrench open a gap in the sliding door of a rail car. It was a narrow space, just wide enough for her slim body to squirm through. Henri handed her a torch and she flicked it on, found whatever wasn't too heavy or tied down, and began pushing it through the gap—cartons of brown eggs from a villager's henhouse, a sack of oats from someone's barn, whole smoked fish that stared at her with glassy eyes, a bolt of woollen cloth that would keep someone warm in winter. When there was nothing more that she could lift, she slipped back through the gap into the night.

"What's left?" Gaston asked.

"Just wine barrels, too heavy to shift."

"We'll siphon the wine off then. Keep watch. If you hear anything, whistle and then roll under one of the trains in the next line over. Don't move until I come to get you."

Gaston used the crowbar again and disappeared into the rail car with a rubber hose, a couple of huge jugs and Henri.

Left alone, Simone began to hear all kinds of sounds, all of them alarming. The night rustled and croaked and hummed around her like a living and malignant creature. Slowly the thrill of the dare began to solidify into a block of ice-cold fear lodged in her chest. Someone had told her once that you couldn't hear bullets until they had already hit you: first the searing of the flesh, then the whistle of the shot, the volley of explosions against the metal of the trains. What was she doing here? She didn't want to get caught. She wanted out now.

She banged on the side of the car.

"Hurry. I hear something—maybe a patrol approaching."

A minute passed, a long, excruciating minute. Then Henri and Gaston were beside her with a half jug of stolen wine and they were running, running fast and low back to the hidden truck.

When Simone felt she could breathe again, she lifted her head from the floor of the truck and found Gaston grinning at her.

"Lost your nerve, didn't you?" he sneered.

"No. I really heard something."

He shook his head and turned away. He didn't believe her. She won no kisses from him that night.

THE LIGHT IN BURGUNDY WAS AMBER in late September, a golden colour the villagers hoped to capture in their wine as they banded together for the harvest, *la vendange*. Despite the burdens of the war, the hunger, the many deprivations, and their own good sense, the villagers were filled with hope. Even Simone could feel the excitement.

Talk at the breakfast table was filled with plans.

"I've volunteered to help at Pommard," Papa said to Simone. "They're my biggest clients. But you and your mother should help in the village."

"Of course. We'll go to the Latours. Pierre can come too."

The little boy clapped his hands. "It'll be like a picnic."

"It'll be hard work," Simone cautioned. "But you can ask Augustine to pack a picnic basket."

While Pierre ran to the kitchen, Simone studied her mother, who had remained silent. Though her performances were predictable, they were always worth studying. Madame Benoir began to toy with her food, her fork making aimless circles on her plate, slowly pushing the food to one side. "Is it far," she asked finally, in a thin voice, "to the Latour estate?"

"Not far. It's next to the chapel at the bottom of the village. But it's not really an estate—just a house, a stable, and a small courtyard. And five hectares of vines."

"Five hectares? You know, Simone, you might be a burden. You've never worked in the fields before and those cutting tools are quite sharp. I wouldn't want you to hurt yourself."

"How hard can it be, Mama? Women have been helping in the fields for centuries."

"Yes, but not women from Paris."

Silence. Papa and Simone dared not look at each other. They waited patiently.

"All right, then. If you're determined to go, I'll just change my clothes."

Madame Benoir stood up from the table with dignity. Simone and her father listened while she crossed the dining room floor. They heard her cross the living room and start up the stairs. They heard her fall and shriek.

Simone had to put a hand over her mouth to smother her laughter, but Papa rose obediently. "Off you go," he said with a wink. "No doubt I'll have to carry her to her bed."

By the time Simone and Pierre arrived at the Latours, the harvesting was in full swing and Gaston was nowhere in sight. Eugénie was happy to see her and pulled her into the kitchen while Pierre ran into the vines.

"Augustine packed whatever she had on hand," Simone said, handing Eugénie the basket. "But she's promised a cake and some pies for later in the week."

"That's generous. Do you want to help here? Everyone will come back for lunch and they'll be starving."

Simone looked around the kitchen. Pots were bubbling and the air was steamy. "I thought, if it's okay, well, I'd like to try picking. I've never had the chance before."

Eugénie smiled and handed Simone a basket and an odd looking tool with a curved blade and wooden handles. "They're called secateurs. Cut the cluster of grapes high up, at the stem. Don't let the grapes fall to the ground. If you hang the basket over one arm and cut with the opposite hand, the grapes will fall into the basket. When your basket is full, just call out and one of the men will come and collect the grapes. Good luck, city girl."

Across the rows of vines, Simone could see Léa and the marigold girl. She waved to them and then settled to work. The grapes hung low on the vine. She had to stoop to find them, and brush back the leaves of the plant to locate the stems of the fruit. The stems were tougher than she thought they would be. The wooden handles of the secateurs chafed her skin. The first cluster of grapes missed the basket and fell to the ground. She looked around quickly, but no one had noticed. She tried again and missed again. She put the basket on the ground and held onto the grapes before cutting the stem. That seemed to work, but it meant she had to crawl along, inching the basket forward. After an hour, her basket was finally full but her cutting hand was blistered and her back ached.

She reappeared sheepishly at the kitchen door. For a moment, she just stood there, watching Eugénie, remembering how unkindly Gaston had described her: plain and spinsterish. Simone saw a square face, handsome rather than pretty, with dark, heavy-lidded eyes and a large mouth with a tendency to lift only on one side when she smiled, if she smiled at all. Her figure was tall, rail straight and angular, but she had a way of moving that was fluid. Her life was hard, her world narrow. She had none of the privileges that Simone had been born to, but she seemed at peace. A whole lifetime spent in Volnay was beyond Simone's imagining, but perhaps it wasn't for Eugénie. Perhaps, for her, it was a blessing to belong, to be part of something, part of the rhythm of the land that not even war could alter.

Eugénie looked up and Simone held out a blistered hand.

"I think you have to be born to it," she said.

Eugénie smiled her crooked smile and held up a spoon.

It wasn't so bad, working in the kitchen. Simone learned many of the tricks of French cooks and the magic that could be performed with fresh herbs. Lunch, when all the pickers gathered around long tables set under the trees, was the picnic Pierre had hoped for. Gaston flirted and winked at her. Despite everything they had endured since the war began, laughter slid as easily up the throats of the villagers as the wine slid down.

At dusk, the sky was almost purple and the air was cool. Simone walked home with Pierre and held his hand. She hadn't thought about Andres all day.

The harvesting might have remained one of Simone's best times in Volnay had it not been for the accident on the third day. She was stirring a sauce in the kitchen, when suddenly she heard yelling and shouting. She looked through the window to see a blur of motion in the vineyard, men running from every corner, leaping over the plants, racing towards the cart that held the bulk of the grapes.

Eugénie dropped the pot she was holding and began running too, Simone right behind her.

At first, she couldn't understand what was happening, except that all the men had their shoulders against the wagon, bracing it on one side.

Then she saw her—Madeleine. She was kneeling beside the fallen horse, its sides heaving, blood pouring from its left haunch. Her golden head was barely an inch from its flailing hooves. She touched the horse, and murmured to it in a sing-song voice. She pulled off her white kerchief and pressed it directly onto the gaping wound. Simone thought she was going to be sick and turned away. All she could see was the bright red blood, the white froth around the animal's mouth and the agony in its eyes.

When she looked across the crowd for Gaston, he was utterly absorbed in tracing every detail of Madeleine's luminous face. Suddenly she knew what had always been obvious to everyone else. Madeleine was Gaston's dark dream. He had never looked at Simone that way, but she knew the expression well. She'd worn it herself when she gazed upon Andres, that obsessive, yearning, hopeless stare that wanted everything and expected nothing. She recognized herself in Gaston, her only ally in Volnay. She recognized the loneliness of reaching for the impossible.

From that moment on, the story of Madeleine and the horse grew, and grew sillier every time. Pierre babbled on about it at dinner.

"You should have seen her, Monsieur Benoir. It was a giant horse and she sang to it, not a bit afraid even though her face was inches from its great hooves, and she pulled the stick right out of its side. She was covered in blood."

"Oh, for heaven's sake, Pierre. It was just a regular old plough horse and she got some blood on the hem of her dress."

"She was brave, though, wasn't she?" he insisted. "Like a princess in a fairy tale."

Simone remembered the silvery night she'd stood alone on a bridge overlooking the Seine with the rain pounding down and the water rushing by. She'd felt the urge to jump run up her legs, but it hadn't reached her heart. She hadn't been brave. She pushed her plate away. She'd lost her appetite.

GASTON WAS ARRESTED IN THE SHIMMERING, tawny yellow of November, 1942. Pierre burst in with the news while the Benoirs were at breakfast. There was a flurry of rumours in the village about what he must have done, but Simone knew the reason, and she knew that her father did too. He would have to intercede.

"I hear he's a troublemaker and a gambler. Women can't stay away from him," Madame Benoir announced.

Simone was amazed that her mother had heard anything about Gaston at all, as she seldom left the house except to hack away at stones and withered vegetables in her garden or go to church. No doubt, the whispers about Gaston would be especially malicious there.

Of course, it was better for her father's reputation not to appear to have a personal motive, so Simone was pleased when Léa and Madeleine came to plead on Gaston's behalf. Pierre was ecstatic to see Madeleine again, the phantom heroine who held him in thrall, but Augustine told him the meeting would be full of grown-up talk and sent him to his room. He looked so dismayed, Simone actually felt sorry for the little brat, especially since she knew the meeting was mere window-dressing. Now her father could move forward with the united and good will of the village.

She accompanied her father to the *mairie* without really thinking there would be much of a problem. Léa and Madeleine had trailed along behind and urged Eugénie to come away with them. Dr. Legard insisted on staying. Simone supposed that her father would be articulate and persuasive, perhaps tell a joke or two. She'd seen him charm the vintners for years. And Gaston would be grateful, happy to see her. Perhaps they would go for a walk afterwards, and he would tell her all about the arrest.

Nothing like that happened.

Beyond the small reception room of the *mairie*, with its innocuous desk and bulletin board, filled mostly with a list of German prohibitions, normalcy ceased. The nameless soldier behind the desk seemed intent on humiliating them. He pointedly ignored their presence and their repeated requests to see the prisoner. They waited and waited, like dogs waiting upon a master. Simone was sick at heart to see her father so belittled.

Finally, an older man arrived, an officer of some kind, Simone supposed. He spoke French and, after a time, a bargain was struck. Monsieur Benoir signed a paper. Simone was allowed to follow the three men down a shadowy corridor to a locked room, but before she could catch a glimpse of Gaston, she was ordered to go no further and wait in the hall. The door opened and shut quickly, exhaling a thick, humid fog that seemed to swallow her up. It stank of urine and blood and fear.

Simone shrank away from the door, leaning against the wall. She opened her eyes to see the soldier from the desk grinning at her, staring at her bare legs and her breasts. She turned her back to him and he swore at her in German, something that sounded as filthy as the smell in the air.

Eventually the door opened and Gaston emerged, dragged forward by M. Benoir and Dr. Legard who balanced his weight between them. His face was battered and his shirt was torn and stained with blood.

Simone was deeply shocked. For the first time, she understood, in her veins and in her heart, the consequences of defying blind authority. She understood that the cards of the future of France were being dealt out by lunatics, thugs, and desperate men. It was pure chance that she hadn't been dragged to this dreadful place herself a few months earlier. Her father looked grim and suddenly old. The doctor looked exhausted, Gaston cowed. This, she thought, is what happens to good men and reckless men alike—an impotency beyond bearing called the Occupation. And what did the Occupation do to women? How many silent degradations and small tragedies of war were left unrecorded? Simone couldn't get out of the *mairie* fast enough.

That afternoon, Simone was glad to be alive. She helped Augustine in the kitchen. She washed the dishes and swept the floor. She made all the beds and played a card game with Pierre. She kissed her father on the cheek after dinner and was an angel of patience with her mother.

"What are you up to now?" Madame Benoir demanded.

Simone just smiled. Her mother always anticipated the worst, managing to find the damp, dark potential in any cloudless sky. But Simone had learned a secret about herself that day. She'd learned that the sharp, fierce anger that rushed through her blood in the *mairie* was stronger than her fear and stronger than her despair. She knew instinctively that anger would heal Gaston's wounds and that the Germans would not break his spirit. Maybe she, too, could use that fire in the blood to burn up her past.

THAT WINTER WAS BRUTAL. Drifts of snow buried the skeletal vines. When the moon turned orange and every windowpane was thick with frost, the people of Volnay turned inward and succumbed to memory.

What Simone clung to during the coldest and loneliest days was her belief that all memory is illusory. There were, of course, things that actually happened where she could pinpoint the day and even the moment. Actual words were spoken, but she'd replayed them so often they'd become a part of her. Had her lover actually spoken these words, or had she longed to hear them so much she'd conjured them up herself?

Time had blunted the edges of things and she couldn't always be sure she got the big, important things right. Her mind seemed to stumble on smaller, particular images. The lilac shawl she wore that first night, slipping from her shoulders. The splash of light rippling on the Seine as the sun was going down.

Mostly she asked herself late at night why it had all turned out the way it had, and why did it have to happen that way. Was it something she said? Was it all lies? Was it something she failed to do or be? Worse, was it something she actually did?

His name was Andres, a teacher of Spanish to a group of unruly and unwilling daughters of wealthy Parisians. From the first time Simone saw him, she could hold only one face in her mind, burning bright in her eyes and torching her heart like swing-jazz music. He held her hand when she was introduced just a moment too long. Their eyes locked and something, some recognition passed between them, as if whatever was going to happen had already been agreed upon.

The pretence of lessons fell away quickly and they met in leafy squares, wine-soaked cafés, elegant parks, and dark corners. His voice had the power to dissolve reality—such a voice, with a light rhythm, as if there was a song already in it. When he spoke Spanish, she could see the dancing that broke out on the streets just because people were glad to see each other and couldn't contain the music inside them. She could hear the soft murmurs of the sea, and smell the salt air of Barcelona. When he kissed her, she could taste Spanish wine flooding her mouth, and when he touched her, Spanish sun melted her limbs.

The civil war in his country had seared his heart and smashed his life into pieces. When the sky over Barcelona had turned scarlet, he'd staggered from the rubble of his home onto a fishing boat and the sea had carried him to France. Eventually, he washed up in Paris. He suffered with every report of executions in Spain and believed the death toll was not the ten thousand reported in *Paris Soir*, but ten times that. His dreams were loud with the voices of the dead. From the corner of his eye, he could see the winds of misfortune gathering on the horizon.

Simone listened to everything and wanted to kiss away every hurt. She wanted to be the light that would glow in his life and banish the shadows. She dreamed of giving him wings that would lift him above his sorrows, so high into the sky the wind would blow away his pain.

After weeks of flirting and dreaming, everything happened so fast that real time seemed to vanish. Andres took her to a bluesy jazz club on the Left Bank. She leaned toward him and listened to his Spanish laments, but when he asked her to dance, the dance was something much more. Erotic. Spellbinding. It was the kind of dance that could make you want things you hadn't even known existed. It made you yearn for more, especially when the last note of the wailing saxophone faded and you were left standing still in someone's arms.

On the walk back to Andres' room, her heart was beating like thunder. She was unschooled in sex. She was a little afraid of sex, but she'd seen enough movies to know that she was walking towards it. She had no loving or instructive words from her mother to guide her so she just listened to her body instead.

The door closed behind her and Andres stood before her. Kissing him would be an invitation, an offering, an unmistakable sign. And so she kissed him, pulling off his cap and her shawl—oh, how she would remember that shawl slipping from her shoulders and puddling at her feet as she slipped off her shoes. She undid her garter belt and rolled down her stockings. She wanted the feel of her bare legs around him.

Blind, beyond thought, her mouth searched for him, finding his mouth with such scalding relief.

The reality of him overwhelmed her—his weight, his smell, his body, so tight and muscled, coiled with power and need. Surely this must be love. A person must love to be so open, so vulnerable, every inch of her skin wanting every inch of his skin, the only man she'd ever known, the fullest, richest being who had ever come into her life.

She left him at night, well before dawn, not just to avoid her parents' knowing. She was afraid the things they said and did would all melt in the light.

Simone fell right off the edge of her life. She dreamed of Andres. She breathed him. She spent every minute she could with him, and when she wasn't with him, she missed him. She missed his moustache and the way he held his cigarettes, the way his black hair curled at the back of his neck. It was hard for her to pay attention to anything else, to focus on anything other than him.

Most of all, she told lies to be with him. She lied to her parents that she was with her girlfriends. She lied to her girlfriends that she was with her parents. That was the trick about lying.

Once she began, she had to do it again and again, trying to remember all the invented intricacies that would make the lie believable to whomever she had to tell lies. The best she could hope for was to tell the same lie to the same people.

At first, the changes in Andres were almost imperceptible, small enough that Simone could explain them away or pretend they weren't happening. He had an extra class to teach and couldn't meet her. She would begin telling him of some little thing that had made her laugh during her day, and he would turn away impatiently. The small slights and petty criticisms began to accumulate, drops of rain gathering into a storm.

When he was making love, Andres was both intensely present and inaccessible. There, and yet removed. Confused by conflicting signals, Simone darted this way and that, and tried to put her unease into words.

"You have such a small vocabulary, my dear," Andres said wearily.

Simone turned her face into the pillow on his bed. Was he talking about her Spanish or her love-making skills? She was too insecure either to ask or defend herself.

Andres never had any money. Simone surprised him with little gifts, frivolous things that would please his vanity, but not hurt his pride: a cigarette case, a bottle of champagne, a scarf of cashmere.

"Truth be told," Andres whispered to her one night while music from a record player drifted over their bodies, "your gifts betray your class. What have your fancy schools taught you of politics, or of the plight of the poor? You're an innocent. What do you know of the stench of poverty?"

Simone couldn't protest. She'd gone to expensive schools at her mother's behest, but not the sort of schools that encouraged a girl to trust her intelligence, value her brains over her beauty, or ponder ethical issues. She'd been nurtured to be decorative, and to turn away from all that was indecorous. She was a pampered flower, protected from every blight and icy wind.

Andres took upon himself the task of educating her. Simone was plunged into a bewildering world of war and politics where human cruelty never failed either to surprise or disappoint. It was as if her happy corner of the world was suddenly bleached of colour, its laughter smothered, its fullness of shape flattened to bitter choices in black and white. Once blind, her eyes watered from all they were now forced to see.

Paris, she saw, was a hard and heartless city, filled with broken veterans with pinned up trousers and an empty space where once there'd been a leg. In the narrow alleys behind expensive restaurants, rats and ragged children scrabbled for scraps tossed into rubbish bins. In Montmarte, in the cafés amid the shadow of Sacré-Coeur, bar-room philosophers, delirious with political theories, promised to change the world, while weary prostitutes paid for their liquor bills.

Simone couldn't eat for guilt, or sleep for the ghosts of Andres' family trapped in a labyrinth of shacks in Barcelona, set ablaze by Franco's soldiers. The elegant apartment overlooking the Bois de Boulogne was a crass announcement of bourgeoisie privilege. Her parents embarrassed her. Her cousins seemed witless and covetous.

Simone stopped spending money on frivolous gifts. She gave Andres all of her allowance now in cash, and pestered her father for more. But it was never enough.

The lies came thick and fast. The pearls her grandmother had given her for her eighteenth birthday? Lost in the Métro. Her gold and ruby birthstone ring? Slipped off her finger and down the drain when she was washing her hands.

Once Simone had been baptized into the gospel of Andres, he began asking her about the party for her parent's twentieth wedding anniversary. He traced the outline of her lips as they lay together in bed. How many people would be there? Who was coming?

"Why?" Simone asked. "Surely you don't want to come."

"No. Impossible. But, you're going to the party, aren't you?

Surely there'll be lots of obscenely rich people there. Just slip something into your pocket, something I can trade for cash. Snatch a bauble or two."

Simone laughed, but Andres was serious. The word *snatch* stuck in her mind, a mean word, reminding her of a low thief who came up behind and punched hard.

"I can't do that, Andres. Whatever you and I might think of these people, they're my parents' friends and family. My family, too."

"Of course, pet. I understand where your loyalties lie." He turned away from her and closed his eyes.

Listening to his breathing, Simone knew that Andres was only feigning sleep. She wondered whether she should beg his forgiveness, or simply leave. She did neither. She remained there, motionless, gazing at the curve of his back and feeling a dark force gathering inside her, whispering that no one would notice a few missing things. Those people already had so much. Andres had nothing, only her. She never said *I love you*, but maybe if she did this thing, he would know.

On the night of the party, the windows of the elegant apartment overlooking the Bois de Boulogne blazed, spilling light and gaiety across the leafy trees and trimmed paths below. A young, love-struck girl stood alone in the cloakroom just off the vestibule, surrounded by cast-off shawls and discarded purses. She reached out her hand and hesitated for a moment. It was a moment she would remember, a moment when the future was not quite set, still a river of possibilities, right or wrong, forward or back, up or down. She looked back, behind her, but no one was watching. She looked down at the glittering brooches used to fasten shawls and the evening purses stuffed with crisp French francs. She lied to herself that no one would care, and she was wrong.

THAT SPRING WAS SO COLD, the eggs of birds froze in their nests. Cold lashes of rain pelted the vines, and all the songs of the birds were mournful. But summer persevered, sunny and benevolent. The vines flourished and Volnay finally shook itself awake from the gloom of bad weather and cold memories. There was good work to be done in the fields, mouths to feed, and stories to tell. The rhythm of the land was implacable, stronger than sadness, stronger than the Germans.

One Sunday in June, the kneeling in church seemed to last for hours. Outside the day smelled like flowers, a sweet rainy smell. Inside the old priest flung his arms about and stirred up the smoky fires of hell. The villagers didn't look like sinners to Simone. Some wore too much makeup perhaps, and some might drink or gamble too much. But sinners? Sinners lied and lusted and stole. She wondered why the villagers came every Sunday and sat so obediently while the priest fixed them with a steely gaze and harangued them from the pulpit.

"Sinners," he warned. "Do you know what Hell is? Hell is the place where God isn't. In the whirlwind of confusion created by sin, listen for a sound. That sound is God, and you will hear it, if you will set aside your sloth and your gluttony and your pride."

Simone listened for the sound. After all, one thief had been saved on Golgotha. Why not her? Yet all she heard was the shuffling of restless feet and the shifting of backsides on the hard pews. She considered she was already in a kind of hell anyway. Some things had to be paid for long after they were found to be worthless.

After mass, the parishioners stood around talking, as if they hadn't seen each other every day for all of their lives. There was Armand Valleray on his mother's arm. She had told everyone who would listen, and many who would have preferred not to, of her son's glorious future. It was impossible to see him as the once-upon-a-time seducer of the village beauty, so elegantly did the robes of impending priesthood float about him. Shame really. He'd have made a malleable husband. And the village beauty? Like a lone star, she'd burned through the bright air and fallen to earth and she never came to church anymore.

Simone's mother flitted about on the edge of the crowd. She was wearing a hat with a little veil that half-covered her eyes, and a full-skirted dress, royal blue, with long sleeves, far too chic for Volnay. She looked like one of the transplanted flowers that she was always trying to coax into bloom in her doomed garden. It was one of those moments that makes the heart stop, when a daughter sees her mother as a separate person and wonders what her dreams once were, what other life she might have lived that would have made her happy. Simone trembled with a longing to touch her, smell her skin, feel the texture of her hair. She took a step forward, but her mother lifted her chin just then, as if aware she was being watched, and turned away from the congregation, heading home, already gone.

Simone exchanged glances with Gaston, but the real Gaston didn't come here. Like her, he pretended. She counted the young men on one hand. They were melting away like morning mist over the dewy grass. Even the dullest among them could see that Vichy's plan to exchange workers for POWs was ludicrous.

Suddenly, she heard shouts and turned her head towards the town square. The gathering outside the church held its communal breath.

Dr. Legard was being marched across the square, wedged between two burly men in the uniforms of the Milice, with Léa trailing helplessly behind. She raised her stricken face to the congregation as she passed and the villagers reacted as one.

There was a low grumble at first, slowly deepening into a growl, the sound an animal might make as it contracts its muscles before lunging forward. One person took a step and the whole group moved. People began running from the café and the surrounding houses to join them. The group became a crowd.

Someone yelled out, "Vichy scum."

The insult was like a stick of dynamite tossed into the air.

The crowd ignited, shouts coming from everywhere.

"Shame."

"Filthy collaborators."

"Bastards."

The Vichy police kept moving, their backs to the crowd, down the hill to the bottom of the village, past the chapel, along the unpaved road that led to Pommard.

A buzzing swept through the crowd like a cloud of angry bees. Pommard meant the doctor would be locked up in the *gendarmerie*. It meant the charge was serious, and even a bribe might not be enough to set him free. Simone thought of her father—he was in Pommard with Pierre today. She hoped he might intercede, but after what she'd witnessed when Gaston was arrested, she feared any attempt would be hopeless.

The crowd grew desperate. From somewhere in its midst, someone pitched a stone into the air. It landed with a thud, squarely on the back of one of the Vichy men.

He whirled around to face the crowd, his pistol drawn, his face expressionless. Léa, at the front of the crowd, was only steps from him.

Simone had never been so frightened as she was when she saw the man's face. There was no sign of fear or anger, no sign at all of any human emotion—just a blank, a terrifying absence.

The policeman threw an arm around Léa's neck and pressed the gun to the side of her temple.

Dr. Legard sank to his knees. "Please. Let her go, please. I'll come quietly. These people will go back to their homes."

The policeman lowered his gun, released Léa, and pulled Dr. Legard to his feet. The march to Pommard resumed as if nothing terrible had almost happened. The crowd had lost its bravado now, but no one went home.

At the *gendarmerie*, both Léa and the doctor were pushed inside, the door shut firmly in the face of the onlookers. They milled around, angry now at their own impotence. Simone decided to find her father and had just turned away from the crowd, when she saw someone running, a blur of movement, a flash of marigold.

Madeleine Vernoux hovered on the edge of the crowd. Her hair was pulled back into a knot that bared the curve of her neck. She was wearing an old-fashioned, simple cotton dress, too long for her, and her arms and feet were bare. Her perfect skin was slightly flushed from the effort of running and her green eyes wide with alarm for her childhood friend. Simone gaped at her. She looked as if she had fallen into their midst from another century. The crowd turned its attention to her, as if she wielded almost a magnetic pull in a moment of suspended time.

A child's terrified cry ripped through the air, shaking the crowd from its stupor. People said that abandoned cats howling in the night sounded like babies crying. But the real thing couldn't be ignored. It was a cry no human heart could turn aside. Madeleine was running again, pulled forward by that pitiable sound.

When Simone reached the top of the lane, she cried aloud and almost fainted with shock for the child was Pierre, trapped in a doorway by a vicious-looking dog. It was the ugliest dog Simone had ever seen, the sort of dog used for fighting. Its ears and tails were cut to nubs, its body thin and scarred.

Simone looked around wildly, but her father was nowhere in sight. She grabbed Gaston's arm, the nearest to her, and pleaded for help.

Slowly, Madeleine took a step forward and the beast lunged towards the child. Pierre screamed, but Madeleine just kept walking, her head swaying slightly, her hands open, her arms outstretched. When she reached the dog, she sank to her knees, placing one hand on Pierre and the other on the dog's mouth.

Pierre had stopped crying, but was rigid with fear, completely motionless. He gazed at Madeleine, transfixed by her face and the power of her touch.

Suddenly the dog's jaw released the child and its head turned to Madeleine. Simone could see the woman's lips moving, whispering something, but could hear nothing. Without warning, the dog turned toward the crowd and came racing toward them. For a wild moment, Simone thought that Madeleine had commanded the dog's fury and unleashed it against the crowd for all its meanness, for all its snide glances that had turned her into an oddity, a living wonder.

A single shot rang out and the dog crashed to the ground with one piercing yelp. Simone thought the bullet must have hit Madeleine too, somehow, for she staggered back and her face winced with pain. Then she turned away quickly to lift Pierre and gather him into her arms, one hand staunching the wound on his thigh.

As Madeleine walked forward, carrying the child, the crowd parted before her and closed in behind her. Simone could not hear what she said to the Vichy man, but clearly one glance into Madeleine's green eyes, green with the unfathomable depths of the sea, was enough.

The crowd dispersed, everyone talking excitedly about their own version of the drama. Simone's father finally panted up to the *gendarmerie* where Simone was waiting for the doctor to finish dressing Pierre's wound.

"What happened?" he gasped.

"You wouldn't believe me, if I told you," Simone replied.

She didn't understand it herself. She didn't want to know why she suddenly cared that a mangy dog could howl like a lost and beaten soul. She didn't understand how Madeleine could be so certain of herself and make others feel so uncertain. All she knew for sure was that her life was running through her hands like water, and she resented the girl who made her remember that. Whenever she was near Madeleine, she felt a flood of emotions rushing through her so fast she could hardly keep her head above water. The fact is she envied Madeleine. She seemed to do whatever she pleased in plain sight, consequences be damned.

Pierre healed quickly, as the young often do. Nonetheless, Monsieur Benoir felt obliged to return with him to Paris in order to allow the boy a visit with his mother. Simone suspected there was a little guilt at play here too, for her father had never adequately explained where he had been in Pommard or why Pierre had been left to wander off alone.

Just after breakfast, her father tapped her on the shoulder. "Are you ready?"

"You're taking me with you? To Paris?"

"It seems the kindest thing to do."

The three travellers left before Madame Benoir could wake up and dash all their plans.

SIMONE COULDN'T BELIEVE HER LUCK and, as far as she was concerned, the train couldn't go fast enough. But her happy mood soured when she learned they would be forced to ride third-class, shoulder to shoulder with people unmistakably suffering from the shortages of soap and laundry detergent.

The train clattered and groaned and seemed to stop at every dusty, sleepy station along the way. Across from Simone, a woman in her fifties with two chins and an untidy nest of greasy hair stared disapprovingly at her pretty clothes. Her father hid behind his newspaper, and Pierre's head slumped against her shoulder. At one stop, a soldier boarded the train, his uniform signalling an instant and uneasy silence. The fat woman reluctantly gave up her seat, as if it were the soldier's right to sit, and shuffled off down the aisle.

The soldier smiled at Simone, lit a cigarette, and blew smoke in her face. She turned away, gazing out the window at the ripening fields and the small circles of houses clustered around church spires in the distance. She wondered how much of the harvest would find its way into French stomachs. How many people in those houses crouched in fear?

Once again, she felt the train grind to a stop. Priority on the rails was given to a line of boxcars running parallel to the passenger train. Suddenly, as the cattle train rumbled by, Simone saw a small hand squeeze between the slats, stretching towards her as if imploring her help.

Simone was stunned, her spine rigid, her breath stopped.

It was just a glimpse, a flash of movement. She might have been mistaken. She must have imagined it. But she knew none of that was true. There were children on that cattle train.

Her head snapped away from the window and her eyes met those of the soldier, dark and pitiless as a frozen sea. He was watching her, she knew, and had registered her alarm. She smelled danger in the air like a charge of cordite, and hugged Pierre close.

FINALLY, PARIS. SIMONE FELT LIKE she'd been anaesthetized in Volnay.

She ran up the steps of the Métro station on the Champs-Elysées ready to embrace the city, full of anticipation. She could already smell the chestnuts in blossom, feel the cobblestones beneath her feet, and see the sweep of the grand boulevards spilling with light and beautiful people.

But Paris had not waited for her. The city had changed in her absence. The streets were grim under a harsh sun—the light sharp, confusing, wrong. The city had a different scent. The heady mixture of exhaust, coffee, baking bread, and the barest whiff of perfume was replaced by the sour smell of fear. It was pressed into the walls and trapped in the streets. It lurked around corners and twitched at the curtains of windows. Bicycle bells replaced the roar of cars. There were no birds anywhere.

The way people walked in the streets looked unnatural. Some of them looked like somnambulists, dragging along, heads bowed, pretending not to see the German soldiers who sat in the cafés or roamed the streets in packs. Others walked too quickly, sharp glances thrown over their shoulders every few yards. The faces of the beautiful people were too thin. Their eyes darted away from Simone, refusing contact, suspicious and wary.

Parisians, Simone realized, averted their eyes as if seeking to insulate themselves from the world and its relentlessly bad news of unexplained disappearances, SS death squads, merciless reprisals, and an anonymous child's hand thrust between the boards of a cattle car, because once people saw, really saw and admitted to the truth of any of these terrible things, they would surely turn to stone or pluck out their eyes or die of shame.

Yet there was still a current of electricity in the air. Not the spark of excitement Simone remembered, but a kind of perpetual, uneasy alert. Paris was waiting, waiting and watching, like some magnificent beast crouching in the dark, ready to spring and snap its jaws, ready to shake off its chains.

Simone slid behind a table in a café she'd often visited with Andres. She ordered coffee and the waitress brought her a thin, brownish liquid with a scum on the top.

"I remember you," the waitress said. "You used to come here with that Spanish man."

"Yes, a long time ago. Where are all the birds?"

The waitress shrugged one shoulder. "They've been eaten. The pigeons first, then even the song birds."

"It's been that bad?"

"Worse. Why have you come back? I thought you'd run away with your lover."

"That was the plan. But it didn't work out. I've been in the countryside."

"Is there food there?"

Simone had an apple and a bar of chocolate in her purse meant to keep Pierre quiet on the train, but he'd slept all the way. She fished them out and pushed them across the table. "Here. Take them. What's your name?"

"Marie." She scooped up the food and hid it in her apron. She turned to walk away, but then changed her mind and offered Simone a worn but clean handkerchief.

"What's this for?" Simone asked.

"You've been away, so you don't understand. You look healthy and your clothes are nice. You should wipe off your lipstick, and don't talk to any Germans. Otherwise you'll be mistaken for a collaborator."

Simone accepted the advice and walked away from the café on trembling legs. She felt self-conscious, as if everyone were looking at her with doubts. She was overcome with nostalgia for the apartment overlooking the Bois de Boulogne, and all the comfort and protection it had once afforded her. She was to meet her father there in two hours, but she couldn't wait that long.

She rode the Métro to Porte Maillot and strode into the huge park. Here at last, among the green shadows of the trees and the mossy haze of summer, there was a sense of peace. She found a bench near the water and watched the swans gliding on the surface, carving feathery wakes in their path.

She had sat in the same spot the morning after the robbery, pressing into Andres' hands everything that she had stolen. He had kissed her passionately, wiped away the tears of her treachery, and poured praise into her ears. *Think of the poor people who will eat meat tonight and sleep under warm blankets. All because of my brave Simone. Meet me here at twilight. We can build a life together, and never be apart.*

She'd wanted to believe him so badly she'd felt an ache in her chest. All day she'd evaded her parents, every phone call they answered from friends slicing away a fragment of the calm mask she wore to hide her deceitfulness. Slowly, bit by bit, people were beginning to notice things missing—a brooch here, a ring there, a taxi fare that couldn't be paid.

Simone had slithered away at dusk, wearing her best shoes and a travelling cape. She'd waited on the bench and watched the day slide away. Finally the night had curled up around her, light spilling down around her, the sky aglow.

People had strolled by and stared at her. There'd been tears on her cheeks, glistening like rain on wet stone, but the people hadn't noticed. They hadn't wanted to look her in the eye. They'd been gone before that. She'd reminded them too much of their own broken promises and fractured hearts.

Her father had finally found her there, just as he found her now.

He sat on the bench beside her and stared straight ahead. "Bad memories?" he asked.

The memory felt like a sickness now to Simone, not for the sin of stealing, not even for the betrayal of her family, but for the unholy longing attached to all of it, the longing for a worthless man.

Her father accepted her silence. He reached out and held her hand. "There's more evil in one block of this city than you could ever imagine, Simone. What you did was wrong and selfish, but not evil. Pierre's parents are practically starving, despite the food Augustine sends them. That's a crime. They live near a place called Drancy, a stinking place where the evil committed is unspeakable. I think, all things considered, it's time to forgive yourself."

"I'll try. How did you keep me out of jail, Papa?"

"Huge sums of money, and lots of begging." He'd tried to lighten her mood, but Simone didn't even smile.

"Sorry," he tried again. "I told the truth. That you were stupid, led astray by a scoundrel, and that you would be punished."

"And they believed you?"

"They wanted to. They seemed to enjoy the scandal."

"It was a thousand times worse than that, Papa. I would have done anything for him, regardless of who might have been hurt or how much. Can you forgive that? It seemed like a dream, but it was more like a trance and then a curse. I lost more than your trust. I lost me."

Monsieur Benoir hung his head. He understood that his child had lost her innocence and there was nothing he could do but hold her hand and watch the sky fall around them in darkening waves.

After a long interlude, Simone spoke again, softly, tenderly. "Tell me please, is there a woman in Pommard?"

He gathered his courage in the long silence, and said simply, "Yes."

"Do you love her?"

"Yes."

"Will you leave Maman? Will you leave me?"

"What happens is up to your mother, but it's time to come home, Simone. We should be in Paris when the war ends. Don't you feel it? The whole city is waiting to explode."

"I do feel it. I want to come back. But Maman?"

"She is my wife. Her home is with us, if she chooses."

They sat on the bench holding hands, each staring into a separate darkness, neither really believing in a world where love was possible anymore.

SIMONE KNEW THAT THE PATH of her future led away from Volnay and back to Paris. She was impatient to begin her life again, to have a fresh start. But while she was happy to leave, she knew her father was not. He was acting from duty alone, the duty to fight for a better Paris and duty to his wife. For that, he would give up love, and she saw too late in him the model she should have followed.

Madame Benoir was not moved by the same loyalties. Thunderstorms of anger and accusations erupted, and the air turned black and sour. She would not go, she raged, not back to a place where her reputation had been slighted by a selfish daughter. She shunned her husband's arguments and wanted no part of the trials of Paris where Simone had brought her only shame. Her husband shut himself up in his study, writing instructions to his employees, and making banking arrangements with financiers. He travelled one last time to Pommard, and came home broken.

Simone felt conflicted about her mother's refusal to return to Paris. What was there for her in Volnay? Was she refusing merely because she was born to be contrary, or was she truly glad to be rid of her daughter? Would she feel a hollowness in her life without her? Simone told herself that the space she took up in her mother's heart was small, and would easily be filled by Papa's cheques. But she couldn't quite believe it.

Some days, Madame Benoir was at pains to describe to Simone the bleakness of Paris, the lack of food, the multiple arrests that everyone knew about, even in Volnay. *The whole city is going straight to hell. You have to stand in line for hours to buy a miserable bunch of carrots.* She wondered aloud in her daughter's hearing if the apartment left behind hadn't been vandalized already. She speculated on the wisdom of keeping the family business thriving on two fronts, and even praised Volnay where life was duller perhaps, but gentler. Those were the times when Simone could believe her mother still had some shred of love for her and maybe did not want her to accompany her father.

The only person Simone told of her plans was Gaston. Their flirtation had ended some time ago and, somewhat to her surprise, they'd stumbled into something like friendship, bound together by discontent with their fates and a thorough dislike of Volnay. Gaston, she knew, was growing desperate, forced to work in the vineyard as the only way to avoid being swallowed up by a German factory. She winced when she saw the skin of his back raw from hours toiling under a pitiless sun.

"Why not come with us?" she asked. "You hate it here even more than I do. You don't want to be a farmer."

"My birthright," Gaston sneered. "It's what the twins wanted, but never me. The vineyard might as well be a prison."

"Well, then, sell it, or at least your part in it. Papa will buy it. He invests in lots of vineyards and surely Eugénie could use the cash."

"You think money will solve everything."

"It has so far. At any rate, it's better than whining. What have you got to lose?"

"I'd never get the travel documents. It's hopeless."

Simone rapped her knuckles on the side of his head. "Use your brains, Gaston. You did the Milice a big favour when you shot that dog, remember? They can get documents for you from the Germans. Especially if Papa gives you a job in Paris."

"Your father doesn't like me."

"No, not much. But he likes me."

"You make it sound so simple. But it's just a dream. Eugénie would never agree to sell even my third of the vineyard. I've asked her before. There are all sorts of legal entanglements preventing the division of the estate, and she has this holy mission to preserve everything for Julien."

Simone sat with her head propped up on her elbows and tried to puzzle out a solution. Eugénie was a formidable obstacle, but there must be a way to get her on their side. Anyone could see that Gaston's situation was precarious. Even if he continued working the vines, he could still be deported at any moment. A solution began to materialize slowly in her head, then gathered speed like a runaway horse.

"I know," she crowed. "Tell Eugénie we're engaged."

Simone could see his muscles tense immediately: a man getting ready to run. She laughed aloud. "Don't flatter yourself, Gaston. All we have to do is lie, and we both know how accomplished we are at that. Eugénie will be relieved that your wild days are over, and a little sorry for me. Papa will give her a packet of money as a kind of reverse dowry—to make up for your lost labour. And when we get to Paris, we'll both be free."

Gaston gave her a crooked smile and gathered her into his arms. "I could almost marry you for this," he murmured.

"Please don't," she laughed, disentangling herself from his arms and pushing him away playfully.

IN HER OWN MIND, Simone was already living again in Paris.

She had entered a new phase of her life, parallel to her everyday experience in Volnay, but distinct from it in every way. She was startled beyond measure to almost collide with Madeleine in the lane that ran past the laundry. She'd had no warning of the enduring reality of Volnay, beyond the faint smell of soap and lemons.

Immediately, Simone felt excluded from Madeleine's strange orbit, even while they were having a conversation. Meeting with her was like watching a foreign film with the subtitles erased. Her own questions rang in her ears as accusations, her statements sounded either arrogant or defensive. She blurted out that she was engaged to Gaston and immediately wished she hadn't. It was just a ruse. She tried to stop the words from coming out, but they seemed to have their own momentum.

For no reason that she could decipher, she found herself smoothing down the pleats in her dress. She fidgeted with her hands and ran her fingers through her hair and had to fight the desire to cross her arms protectively over her chest, her body speaking a language all its own.

And all the while, Madeleine remained unshaken, her face beautiful, concerned, and insufferable.

Simone hurried away, forcing herself not to run. What was it about the marigold girl that disturbed her so much? She made Simone feel like she was missing something, some vital piece. It was as if, each time they met, Madeleine pointed a finger at some gap, prodded some bruise, some vulnerable spot.

Simone had even tried to hurt her by speaking Armand's name. "You'll have to give him up," she'd said meanly.

"I already have." Madeleine had replied calmly.

I have? Was it that simple, after all? She'd expected something more melodramatic from Madeleine, some magic spell. If you wanted to erase a man from your heart, say his name backwards three times, perhaps, or write his name on a piece of paper and burn it.

That night, Simone couldn't get Madeleine out of her

thoughts. She was convinced she was trying to tell her something, find something maybe, or heal something. She tried conjuring up Andres in as much detail as she could bear. The spark in his eyes, the rasp of his tongue, the way he walked— long, loping strides, the way he walked away from her, his black coat swinging around his legs. She'd burned for him, stolen for him, lied for him. Now she would burn him from her memory. Perhaps that was Madeleine's magic. She knew how to rise from the ashes.

THE LAST DAYS OF AUGUST left the population of Volnay slightly dazed. The light was golden and warm on the skin. Renegade rain showers sweeping across the landscape left the fields ripe and the grapes plump. White butterflies rose in gauzy clouds above the vines. Even Simone, whose laugh had come back to her when she least expected it, had to admit the days were glorious.

She had never felt so alive. Despite the cold, bitter taste of Occupied Paris, she was ready to face it head-on. She had no desire to be safe, only a determination to run towards her future.

On the last day, at the last moment, she took the most difficult step.

"I've come to say goodbye, Mama."

Madame Benoir, stretched out on a lounging chair, put down her magazine and looked up at her daughter.

"You've always defied me, even in the cradle. You should know that I tried to dissuade your father from letting you return to Paris for your own safety. But I see you're prepared to throw that away."

"Augustine and Pierre will look after you. Papa needs me. Gaston is taking me to the train station in Beaune and I'll meet Papa there."

Madame Benoir stood up and, for a moment, Simone thought her mother might embrace her. She felt a rush of regret for all the storms that had ignited between them, and all the sparks of love that had not.

But Madame Benoir remained motionless, her arms stiff at her side. She merely studied her daughter's face, and Simone felt an unwelcome pity in her gaze.

"You're a fool," Madame Benoir warned, "if you think Gaston will join you in Paris."

"I don't know what you mean. He'll come as soon as his travel documents arrive."

"Don't pretend to be stupid, Simone. It doesn't become you."

Her mother said no more, but she softened at the end and placed one hand, briefly, against her daughter's cheek.

Simone rode to Beaune with Gaston in Henri's old turnip truck. It seemed a fitting way to leave Volnay. She looked out the window of the truck and saw that the vines were acid green in the setting sun. She looked at Gaston and saw the muscles of his jaw tense. Could it be that he was sorry to see her go? He carried her suitcase into the station and hugged her on the platform.

"See you soon," he promised.

Simone watched him, another man walking away. In time, she would learn that a man who keeps promises is as much a wonder of the world as the Eiffel Tower, or as a dance in the arms of an American soldier on Liberation Day, or as a woman she'd once called the marigold girl.

LÉA

WHERE WAS GASTON LATOUR? In typical Volnay fashion where life droned by tediously, where daily routines were repeated at the same slow pace, and where days stuck to one another all the same colour, it took several weeks for the question to reach a fever pitch of curiosity.

No one had seen him at church. The chair he frequently occupied at the local bar remained empty. Several village wives, who wisely chose to remain silent, missed him from their beds. In the offices of the Milice in Pommard, a set of travel documents in his name gathered dust.

Speculation spread across the vineyards, through the windows, and over the thresholds of the village.

He must be hiding out from the Germans at the Latour place.

I heard he's eloped with Simone Benoir.

No, no. He's joined the Resistance fighters.

Eventually, those puffed up puppets wearing the uniforms of the Vichy police whispered into the ears of the Gestapo and soldiers were ordered into action. On their way to the Latour vineyard, the German trucks were a low rumble and their motorcycles a high-pitched whine that roused every household. People nearby swore they could hear heavy German boots thudding across the floor of the Latour barn, across the courtyard, through Eugénie's kitchen and up the stairs into the bedrooms, and even up and down the rows of vines. The Germans poked into every closet, emptied every chest, and defiled every drawer. Angry because they could find nothing and because the village would surely laugh at their miserable failure, the soldiers shouted at Eugénie until their voices were hoarse, but she could tell them nothing, only stand before them with empty hands, staring over their shoulders at a picture of Julien whose image gave her the strength to withstand the onslaught.

By the time the Germans returned to the village, after curfew so that they would not have to bear the sly glances of those who relished their incompetence, it was clear that Gaston Latour had vanished.

In the months that followed, amid the unrelenting conjecture offered up by the villagers—the envious, the frightened, the bored, and the broken-hearted—only three people believed they knew the true story of what had happened to Gaston Latour, and all three were wrong.

WHEN LÉA HAD OPENED THE DOOR and her arms to Madeleine on that fateful afternoon, she could already taste the metallic tang of fear in her mouth, so sure was she that something life altering had happened. She had only to believe the evidence of her senses to guess the worst. Each time Madeleine tried to speak she seemed to gag on her words. Her arms were covered in bruises and her dress was covered in blood. Under her wild hair, one side of her pale face was badly swollen.

Léa immediately took charge, as she so often did when the ailing, the confused, and the desperate came knocking on the doctor's door. She took Madeleine by the hand and led her, as one might guide a blind child, to her bedroom. There, she unbuttoned her bloodied dress and helped her step out of it. She wrapped her in a blanket and brought her a glass of brandy, mixed with hot water and laced with a sedative from her father's supplies.

"You need to rest, Maddy. We can talk later."

But Madeleine would not be stilled. She threw off the blanket and began to pace the room, in erratic, slowly constricting circles. Léa could barely watch. There was something manic about the pacing, as if Madeleine's body seemed to register at the edge of each cycle that there was no place left to go.

Something ugly slipped into the room then, some premonition that had been lurking there for a long time. Léa was not shocked. Some part of her had known this would happen. *Had known* and yet she'd done nothing to protect her friend.

"Gaston attacked you," she said flatly.

Madeleine froze, her head jerked up and her eyes widened and in an unstoppable torrent of words she told Léa all the sordid and ugly details of the attack in the clotted shadows of the barn. "I killed him. I smashed a wine bottle over his head and killed him and now...." Madeleine sank to the floor, her head on her knees, so diminished she looked like a heap of rags.

Léa remained calm, her voice steady, though every nerve in her body seemed to vibrate. "How do you know he's dead? You might have just knocked him out."

Madeleine did not even look up. "No, there was so much blood."

"Did you feel for a pulse? Head wounds bleed a lot."

"It's no use, Léa. I killed him." Madeleine staggered to her feet. "I'll tell Papa first. The shock will kill Mama. Then maybe your father can take me to Pommard to the police. And Eugénie. She mustn't find him when she's all alone. Someone has to warn her."

Madeleine's final words were slurred. Léa stepped forward and took the glass of brandy from her hand, coaxing her toward the bed. When Madeleine finally tumbled into it, Léa covered her with the blanket again and smoothed her hair from her face.

No one knew Madeleine better than Léa. She could see right through to her soul. And she knew her friend was too transparent, incapable of deception.

Léa sat down on the edge of the bed and considered the deep, strange difference of Madeleine: her unsettling beauty, her disregard for convention, her indiscriminate compassion. Lots of people thought she was crazy, believed her otherworldliness was a form of lunacy. Her difference frightened them. However extraordinary she was, in this she was perfectly ordinary. She would be judged harshly, with suspicion and mean-spirited resentment. Her beauty was just another way to discount her, to set her apart, to not see who she truly was.

Léa had assumed, wrongly and dangerously, that Madeleine's goodness could prevent disaster. Now she knew she could not save Madeleine from what she had done, nor from what Gaston must have done to her to deserve it, but she could save her from the consequences. She knew exactly what she must do. She was prepared, this once, to risk everything.

JUST BEFORE SOLANGE LEGARD LEFT this earth forever, she called her husband to her bedside and made him promise that Léa would not have a melancholy childhood. The good doctor kissed his wife goodbye, closed her eyes for the last time, and kept his promise. Though Léa missed her mother like all little girls would, she was a happy child because her father's love filled up all the rooms of their house.

Léa had lovely dark eyes and rosy cheeks, but everyone agreed her smile was her best feature. It lifted her father up from his sorrow and gave him a reason to live. Under his attentive eye, Léa grew in leaps—standing one day and running the next, babbling incoherently then suddenly speaking in complete sentences. Her father rocked her cradle to the rhythm of the lullabies he sang into her ear. He taught her how to tie her shoes and how to hold a fork and, when her legs were long enough, how to ride a horse.

A small group of village women took it upon themselves to cook and clean for the Legards on a neighbourly basis. They called Léa *mon ange* and spoiled her every chance they had to compensate for the fact that she could not be spoiled by her own mother. They took turns braiding her silky black hair into a single, long plait that swung down her back and they took care that her face and hands were always clean.

In return, Léa loved the village—the old stone houses, cherry trees that blossomed in the spring, the stubborn vines, the flowers that somehow managed to grow over the stone fences of the *domaines*. She even loved the bleating goat in Armand's mother's parched yard, and the old men who still wore berets, and reeked of Gitanes and red wine. She held a special fondness for mothers who would hang out their bed sheets to dry and, no matter how burdensome their chores, find time to play with her and maybe slip a sweet biscuit into the pocket of her dress.

At bedtime, Léa's favourite stories were always about her mother who looked regal under a white parasol in a photograph kept by her bed. She would pester her father for details to nourish her dreams, but no story was ever enough to make a whole picture. Sometimes, she imagined her mother as an angel looking down upon her from a cloud in the thin, brilliant air. But as a doctor's daughter, even as a child, Léa knew enough about ailments, fevers, accidents, and gnawing illnesses to suspect that the dead were gone forever and not floating about in the sky anywhere.

As she grew older, she put aside childish versions of her mother and replaced them with flesh and blood stories of a woman named Solange who stood steadfastly by her husband's side in make-shift medical tents, trying to stitch together French boys cut apart in a hail of bullets amid the anguished landscape of the Great War. Léa preferred this mother, and knew that her hands were gentle, her words were kind, and her heart was brave. She planned to be just like her and so she did not dwell on the past, but busied herself with the emergencies of the present.

The most dreadful of those emergencies was the unwanted arrival of the Germans in Volnay and the humiliating defeat of France. Now, after three years of occupation, Volnay was an island of despair, cut off from the larger world by a lack of information and buried under a mountain of decrees. In the heart of the country, the villagers were relatively safe from the drone of the bombers and the destruction that rained down from the sky. But the enemy could be anywhere, sliding up next to you in a black Mercedes with swastika flags, or hiding behind the false smile of a neighbour. Every hidden radio and stolen scrap of food could be a death warrant. Every hunting rifle stashed in a *cave* could trigger an execution. Léa shuddered to remember the arrest of her father, how close she had come to losing him, and the risks they continued to take together.

But what hurt her most was the change in the children. It was not just that they were hungry, with pinched faces and matchstick limbs, but that they were learning to fear and to hate. Only three years ago, they had been ordinary, adventurous, and pure of heart, playing in the village square, squirming in church, and stealing apples from neighbours' orchards. Now they moved cautiously, warily, as if bombs were buried under their feet. They no longer jumped or shouted outdoors. That brought attention to you, and attention brought you the gaze of a Nazi. They saw the way grown-ups shuffled past the Germans with averted eyes and so they learned it was best to practise becoming invisible. They read the German posters that promised to feed them milk, bread, and jam, but all the Germans really put into their mouths were vile names for Jews and saboteurs. When Monsieur Rosen disappeared from the schoolhouse late in 1942 and Léa stepped in to take his place, little Giles Drouhin said he was glad because the teacher was a filthy Jew. It was the saddest sound that Léa had heard in almost three years of sorrow.

LÉA FIRST SAW MADELEINE AS A SHIMMER of light, a translucent shift beside the lavender that her mother had planted long ago in the Legard garden. As Léa stared, Madeleine had darted from her hiding place and run toward the cherry tree, climbing it as easily as if she were mounting a flight of stairs. Her face poked out from amid the branches, an exotic blossom blown wildly off course. "Come and play," she'd said and so began the abiding friendship that would alter the course of their lives.

Léa knew why she loved Madeleine. Whenever she looked into her face, the season became summer and the sky grew larger and she felt as if she was living a life of perpetual surprises. With Madeleine by her side, Léa felt she could do anything or be anyone. Borders and possibilities expanded and the unexpected beckoned.

Their childhood was spent together in a seemingly never ending summer of long days and abandon. One day, they would defy gravity, running along the tops of the stone fences that divided one vineyard from another, arms spread wide to keep their balance, ready for anything. On another day, they might ride Léa's horse bareback through the village square, then slide to the ground convulsing with laughter. They experimented with baking as a surprise for Léa's father, producing a series of misshapen cakes amid clouds of flour and wafts of smoke. The doctor proclaimed each one delicious, but Madeleine later told her own Papa that they tasted mostly of sugared paste and chickweeds.

Some days, the two little girls would simply lie in the grass under the endless arc of the sky, while Madeleine concocted thrilling and completely unbelievable stories of trees that could move about freely in the forest when the moon was at its fullest, or of sleek mahogany horses that could run so fast they seemed to set the earth beneath their hooves on fire, or of sailors who swore they had beheld a host of naked women skimming over the waters of the sea and so had willingly blinded themselves because no future sight would ever be as glorious.

Madeleine's imagination was like a delicate rope ladder that the two friends could climb to impossible heights. Whenever Dr. Legard feared they might float away, he gave them practical chores to do to remind them that their place was here on earth.

It was in the schoolroom when Léa first learned that others did not feel as comfortable around her friend as she did. One day, during a history lesson about French kings, Madeleine, who usually paid no attention, but sat silently gazing out the window or drawing, put up her hand and asked in a clear voice that roused even the sleepiest student: *What colour is God?*

There was a moment of stunned silence. Even Monsieur Rosen, who did his best to shield Madeleine from the frequent stares of the other children, was left speechless and totally incapable of controlling the bedlam that erupted. Some students were shocked. Surely such a question was blasphemous. They pointed fingers and promised to tell their parents. Others nearly rolled on the floor, whooping with laughter at such a silly, stupid girl.

After that day, things grew worse, especially in the playground. But Madeleine didn't seem to need Léa's protection. All the mean words and jibes slid right off her as if she hadn't heard a single insult that had been flung at her. When Gaston Latour threw mud on her dress to see if he could make her cry, she brushed her skirt and put her finger in her mouth to see if the mud tasted like chocolate. She was puzzled by meanness, but unperturbed. Eventually, the bullies learned that there was no fun to be had trying to rattle her and so they left her alone and went back to the task of memorizing the perfect symmetry of her face.

Since leaving school, Léa had had less time to share with her friend, though her affection for her was unconditional. When people maligned Madeleine for her scandalous behaviour with Armand Valleray, Léa turned on them like a tiger, and when Armand himself gave up Madeleine for God and the seminary, she treated him with a politeness so cold that he was in danger of frostbite whenever he came anywhere near her. For Léa knew that despite Madeleine's excesses, she had the touch of an angel about her, an impulse for goodness that ran deep. And that was Léa's reason for wanting Madeleine to live an unfettered life as long as she could, and her reason for keeping secrets.

A LIGHT MIST DRIFTED LIKE A VEIL over the vines by the time Léa returned home. She was relieved to find her father still out, but worried that he worked too hard, always willing to rise in the middle of the night to visit a feverish child, or share the burden of sorrow when a loved one passed. No doubt that was where he was now, sitting with the family of old Grenelle, who had stuffed an abundance of white hair under his beret and waxed the tips of his moustache every day, and whose heart had finally reached the limits of its endurance, suffering under the indignity of the Occupation. Tomorrow, the whole village would walk behind his coffin to the old cemetery beside the chapel and complain that there were no plumed black horses, draped with purple ribbons and black netting, because the Germans had snatched up all the horses. They would reminisce about what a rascal Grenelle had been as a boy, how he had loved to whistle a Maurice Chevalier tune, and pinch the bottoms of pretty girls. They would remember what fine wine he had made. And many would wonder where on earth was Gaston Latour.

Léa changed her clothes and washed her hands and face, before slipping into her bedroom where she had left Madeleine in a drugged and dreamless sleep. She knelt by the bedside and kissed Madeleine on the cheek. Her skin smelled of sorrow and her face was cold, her bruises like purple ink stains running up and down her arms. Léa could hear her breathing, long intakes of breath that sounded like sighs.

"Wake up, Maddy."

Léa waited for Madeleine to open her eyes and could not fail to notice the exact moment when she remembered why she was sleeping in someone else's bed—a dazed expression, like a woman struck by lightning.

"Everything is going to be fine, Maddy. I've been out to the Latour place and Gaston isn't there. He's gone."

Madeleine stared at her friend, disbelieving, wanting so badly to believe her. She shook her head, "That can't be. I told you what happened. I killed him. Did you talk to Eugénie? Maybe she found him. Maybe she's already gone to the police." She threw off her blanket and staggered to her feet. "I have to go now. I have to go to her and beg her forgiveness."

"Sit down, Maddy. Listen to me," Léa ordered.

Madeleine sat down abruptly, surprised to hear such a commanding tone in her friend's voice.

"Eugénie is probably sound asleep. I went to the barn and everything was just as you said. I saw the glass from the broken wine bottles and I even saw blood. But Gaston is definitely gone. I wanted to come straight back to tell you, but I also found Achilles, so I buried him. He's here, in the back garden. You can visit him whenever you like."

Madeleine clung to Léa's every word, but she still couldn't believe what she was hearing.

"I swear he was dead."

"You thought he was dead, that's all. You were in shock."

"Maybe Eugénie wasn't asleep. She might have gone to the police."

"No. Her bicycle was there, leaning against the house. Frankly, I'm not at all surprised that Gaston is gone, after what he did to you. Your Papa would skewer him alive if he saw those bruises on you. It was only a matter of time, anyway."

"What do you mean, a matter of time?"

"Young men are as scarce these days as food, gas, and electricity. Those few who are left are in danger of being arrested or deported every day. Any one of us could disappear tomorrow. Is it so hard to believe that Gaston would run? And you know how much he hated working in the vineyard."

"But he was going to marry Simone."

"And attack you while he waited? I don't think he was hearing any wedding bells."

Madeleine fell silent then, seeming to turn inward. She moved like a somnambulist across the room and picked up her dress from where it had fallen the night before, but when she saw the bloodstains she let go of the soiled cloth and watched it drift back to the floor.

Léa studied her carefully. She wished Madeleine would rest. She wished she would believe her story, but she knew that wouldn't happen until Madeleine saw with her own eyes the scene in the barn exactly as it had been described to her. She could see in Madeleine's posture that the tug of the stable was like a string tied between each vertebra, the only thing keeping her upright.

"All right, Maddy," she said. "I'll take you there. Wear my clothes and I'll saddle my horse."

They rode to the Latour place the way they had often ridden as children, with Léa at the reins, Madeleine's arms encircling her waist. It was only a short distance from the doctor's house, but Léa considered Madeleine too weak to walk and, despite the experience she had gained accompanying her father on medical visits, she couldn't predict what Madeleine's reaction would be to revisiting the site of Gaston's assault. Léa's blood was already thundering through her veins, as the two friends dismounted. She led the way and pushed open the stable door with grim determination.

Madeleine hesitated at the threshold. She lifted her head, as if she could smell something burning, something hot and raw that scorched the very air she breathed. She began to tremble and Léa feared it had been a terrible blunder to bring her back.

It was Jacques who saved the moment. The old horse shook his mane and nickered when he saw Madeleine and she was powerless to resist that call. She ran to him, seeming to pull strength from the powerful depth of his chest and the whiskery velvet of his mouth. But still, she had her back turned to the spot where Gaston had fallen.

"You only have to open your eyes, Maddy, and look," Léa whispered.

Madeleine turned then and her eyes widened. The broken glass had been swept away. The dirt floor of the barn had been raked smooth and dusted with a layer of fresh, sweet-smelling straw. Were it not for the physical evidence of the marks on her skin, Madeleine might have supposed that all that had happened here in the shadows of a lost day was nothing but a malignant hallucination.

The two women rode back to the village the way they had come, but the day seemed brighter and the distance shorter. The air around them seemed to thicken into a deep, concentrated, and melting sigh. As to who had erased every telltale sign of the attack, Madeleine didn't need to ask, nor Léa to tell.

THE SUNDAY AFTER THE BURIAL of old Grenelle, Léa stood by the open church doors and listened carefully to the villagers who, released from the burden of their sins for another week, were eager to share their own versions of the disappearance of Gaston Latour. At first, the questions she'd faced had felt as sharp and dangerous as fishhooks, but now she was beginning to understand what stories her neighbours were willing to accept. Everyone saw what they expected to see and heard what they expected to hear. They found the endings to their stories that seemed most likely to fit the plot and the person they thought they knew. Those who thought well of Gaston, who thought his dark good looks and recklessness had brought a flourish of romance into their placid lives, were convinced that he had joined the underground struggle to restore the glory of France, or at the very least to gnaw persistently at the German ropes that kept the village in bondage. Others who knew of his black market dealings and his careless dalliances with women suspected that his bravado was nothing but smoke that would dissipate in the slightest breeze and that he would most likely be found hiding under a skirt in Paris or behind a rock in the Morvan.

Léa didn't care which version of the story won the day, but she was worried that Eugénie was standing alone, pale and isolated, while the rumours washed over her. Nobody was asking her how she felt, for fear that she would tell the truth. She was a woman alone, with all the labour of a vineyard, few supplies, and no men. How would she cope?

Léa had started to move towards Eugénie when Armand Valleray blocked her path. Amazed that he had the audacity to approach her, she found herself at a loss for words and stared at him mutely.

"I was wondering if you would come to visit my mother."

"Is she sick?" Léa responded, immediately concerned.

"Not exactly."

"Then what, exactly?"

"I'm leaving for Paris tomorrow, back to the seminary. She could use a friend."

"I'll drop in first thing tomorrow morning then. But, Armand, I warn you, I won't hear a word against Madeleine."

Armand flushed at the sound of that name and ran his fingers over the heavy cross that hung around his neck as if he were touching a talisman to ward off evil thoughts. "Where is Madeleine, by the way?"

His effort to make the question sound casual was so forced that Léa almost took pity on him until she remembered the terrible, almost feral grief that his abandonment had caused her dearest friend. "You know she doesn't come to church anymore. She doesn't want to lay eyes on you. And who could blame her?"

Rebuffed, Armand turned as if to walk away, but then changed his mind. "I made my choice, Léa. An honourable choice which I'll not apologize for to you or to her. I'm not alone in wondering where she is. She's not been seen at the Latour vineyard, in the village, in the fields, or even up in the trees, not since Gaston disappeared. I'm not the only one wondering. Perhaps they've run off together. She has a reputation for being impulsive, after all."

"You question *her* reputation?" Léa seethed. "You're a fool, Armand. You were closer to true goodness with Madeleine than you'll ever be in your black cassock. You put her in more danger than you'll ever know. You should be begging the heavens for *her* forgiveness. That would've been the honourable choice."

Walking away, Léa knew she had said too much and, at the same time, not enough. She wanted to shake Armand like a feather duster and make him understand that his faithless romancing of Madeleine had left her vulnerable to men like Gaston. Before Armand, she was locked in the tower of her own beauty. Afterwards, that tower was assailable. Léa wondered if Armand might ever fit her words together with the circumstances and realize what Gaston had done. To calm down, she assured herself that Armand was not the boy he once was, curious and openhearted. He'd become proud and stiff with the assumed status of his new position, blinded by ambition. Whatever small part of him still remembered the lingering scent of Madeleine's hair or the lullaby of her voice, would soon be overpowered by the smell of incense and the chanting of prayers.

Though Léa longed to speak with Eugénie, she had a more urgent errand now. She knew why Madeleine had stayed indoors. She was waiting for her injuries, both visible and invisible, to heal. She was waiting for her bruises to fade and the secret in her eyes to dim. *Gaston was gone.* Léa knew that Madeleine's mind careened around this fact obsessively with little sense of how it could be possible. But, if Armand had been right about anything, he'd been right about gossip. It was time to take a meandering stroll with Madeleine through the village, no matter what state the girl was in. Léa would invent some story, a fall perhaps. She was beginning to realize that some people would believe almost anything.

And so it was on that last Sunday afternoon in August, when people glanced through the lace curtains of their windows or sat in the café in the centre of the village square, drinking cups of bitter *faux* coffee made from ground chicory, they saw the two women walking with their arms encircled and for a moment forgot about the deprivations caused by war and felt instead their hearts uplifted by the tenderness that existed between them.

BECAUSE MADAME VALLERAY WAS A SIMPLE, hard-working woman who had suffered the grievous loss of a husband, Léa had long forgiven her excessive pride in Armand. So the next day, she kept her promise to the would-be priest and made her way through the village to the Valleray house. It was, like many others in Volnay, a humble stone cottage with wooden floors and whitewashed walls, and two windows with green shutters on either side of the front door that opened directly into a large open living room, with a kitchen to the right.

Léa knocked on the door, embarrassed by her empty hands. It used to be the custom for visitors to bring a small jar of jam, or a basket of vegetables or fruit when calling, but there was no food to spare in Volnay. Worse, it seemed as if goodwill itself had withered on the vine, as people forgot the old customs, works of charity, endearments and ordinary friendly politeness, and thought chiefly of their own welfare first, waiting impatiently for the Germans to get on with the business of losing the war.

Madame Valleray's eyes were red and she clutched a handkerchief to her breast, but Léa guessed accurately that her sadness over the absence of her son would soon be soothed by the certainty of his ordainment. Indeed, she forced herself to sit patiently, listening to every detail of the process by which this glory would be attained until she felt that even a saint could not be expected to endure more. Léa rose to leave, but Madame Valleray suddenly changed the focus of her attention.

"And how is Madeleine feeling? Better now?" The question was accompanied by the kind of wan, insincere smile meant to disguise an old lady's intrusive and not entirely benign curiosity as polite concern.

As calmly as she could, Léa replied. "Madeleine's fine. She's not been ill as far as I know."

"No, not ill. But we all know she made such a fuss when Armand heard the Lord's call. I saw her running across the fields and along the road just the other day, running like the devil himself was chasing her, and I thought perhaps she was about to have another of her spells."

"You're mistaken, Madame Valleray. I saw Madeleine just yesterday and we had a lovely walk around the village. She's perfectly fine."

"I'm sure you're right. No one's closer than you two girls. But you might want to ask her about that day she was running. I couldn't help thinking she'd seen or heard something that frightened her near to death. Right around the time Gaston disappeared, I think it was."

The last of Madame Valleray's words lingered in the air and her sharp eyes were fixed on Léa's face, but Léa refused to flinch and stared back impassively.

"Thank you for your concern, Madame Valleray, and for the visit," she replied finally.

The old lady clutched at Léa's sleeve as she reached for the doorknob. "It's only a friendly warning, my dear. Madeleine should be more careful. There are more Germans moving into the area."

"More of them? Why?"

"It's the big house. Now that Monsieur Benoir and Simone have returned to Paris, there are empty rooms. Armand told me that Madame Benoir has been ordered to relocate to the ground floor, near the cook and the little boy. Three Germans are moving into the upper bedrooms. Armand says one of them is a Gestapo officer."

Léa was appalled at the news. Many soldiers were billeted in the surrounding area, but Volnay had been spared that particular indignity because the Germans preferred the more luxurious estates to be found in nearby Rully, Pommard, and Aloxe-Corton. More to the point, the soldiers who regularly patrolled Volnay had grown used to the village and its inhabitants: custom had staled their vision. Volnay was like a familiar picture hanging on a wall to them, something that you saw, but didn't see at the same time. What would new soldiers with new eyes discern? And even though she barely knew Madame Benoir and had listened often enough to Simone's complaints about her, Léa felt true pity for her. No one should have to endure the Occupation in such proximity.

"Will Madame Benoir return to Paris now?" she asked.

"Not her," was Madame Valleray's blunt reply. "She has a bad temper and a selfish heart. I'd say she was a match for any German."

LÉA WENT FIRST TO HER FATHER with the news. She found him at home, which was rare these days. Doctors were scarce and medical supplies even more so. In addition to caring for the villagers, Dr. Legard was often called to Beaune or Chalon-sur-Saône, and sometimes travelled as far south as Lyon to barter for antiseptics or morphine. The Germans had allowed him to keep Léa's horse and his old car, but without gasoline, the car was useless, and even the simplest of journeys, by train or by bicycle or on foot or on horseback, became arduous. Léa worried about him constantly and feared that he was so worn down, he would one day collapse under the burdens that rested on his shoulders.

She gave her father a kiss and coaxed him to sit down long enough to eat some bread and soup. She watched him dip the hard crusts into the soup to soften them and sighed. "Remember when the villagers used to pay you with food? Baskets of eggs, jugs of cream, chickens and whole hams? I've been to see Madame Valleray this morning. She didn't offer any food, but she had news."

Dr. Legard raised an eyebrow. "She's a terrible gossip. Who's caught her eye this week?"

Léa told him about the billeting of the Germans, but said nothing about the sighting of Madeleine running from Gaston, for surely that was what the old woman had seen. "She has a harsh opinion of Madame Benoir and believes she'll stay in the house," she added. "Do you know her, Papa?"

"Not really. I met her when I was tending the boy, Pierre. We've seen her at church. You probably know her better from Simone."

"So there's no need for you to go to the Benoir house?"

"No need, unless I'm called there. I know what you're thinking, Léa. We agreed not to take unnecessary risks."

"But someone should warn them, Papa. The partisans went there for food sometimes, when Gaston was seeing Simone."

"Leave it, Léa. If Madame Valleray knows about the billeting, the whole village will soon know. And who's to say Gaston's not already with the partisans? He'll know that conditions at the house have changed and that their friends have moved back to Paris."

Silence was Léa's only refuge.

THE NIGHT WAS CLEAR AND FULL OF STARS. Far in the distance, bombs were falling. After the deep thumping of the earth stopped, the sky to the east was a brilliant orange. A troop of soldiers hurried past her, a sudden wash of grey on their way to the airfield in Dijon.

Léa stepped out of the shadows and led her horse out of the small stable. The click of the gate was like the snapping of a bone. She paused, watching for any chink of light escaping through the blackout curtains, but she knew her father was exhausted and would sleep until dawn. Slowly, carefully, she moved along the sides and backs of houses. Voices carried in the night through open windows. Somewhere a baby was crying. Pots clattered as the last of the day's meal was cleared away. Beyond the village, the lanes became dirt roads lined with ditches of long, sweet-smelling grass. There she mounted her horse, grasped its mane in her fingers and galloped for the Morvan.

The huge forest, dotted with clear, cool pools and waterfalls, twisting roads, deep gorges, plateaus of lush grass, and craggy outcrops of rock, was no longer a benign retreat where parents brought their children for swimming and Sunday picnics. Now it was a menacing place, the base of the resisters who hid behind the rocks, in caves, and up in the trees. Under the thick canopy of leaves and the towering gloom of the firs, the darkness was like quicksand, swallowing Léa whole. Sounds bounced from rock to rock, amplified by water, refusing to be still.

Sabotage operations by the local resistance groups were of a low, but persistent level—a telephone pole cut down, a thumb tack stuck through a signal wire to jam communications, the occasional tree felled across a road, watered gasoline so that cars would stutter and stall. These pranks were carefully calculated to leave the Germans nervous, and keep them busy and frustrated, but not so alarmed as to carry out reprisals against the village. Still, Léa knew, saboteurs and anyone found helping them were to be shot.

More than the partisans, she feared the packs of wild dogs that roamed the myriad paths. Most had once been pets, abandoned by their owners who, unable to feed them, could not bear to watch them starve. As the dogs grew thinner, every rib visible along their skinny flanks, they grew meaner and more feral. The fights among them drew blood—most had ripped ears and matted coats scarred by bite marks. Those that survived slept all day and ran with the wind all night.

Léa dismounted and stood trembling by her horse. She whistled: a lonely, plaintive sound in the hugeness of the night.

At last, she heard the whistle returned.

Wrapped in a black shawl that covered her head and brow, Léa emerged from the trees like some dark winter bird. She didn't waste time or exchange greetings. She delivered her message and pressed a small package of medicine into the hands of the unshaven, dirty man who had come to meet her, whose stained clothes smelled of pine sap, stale sweat, dampness, and fear.

Then she left the way she had come, her black shawl melting into the thick dark ahead.

Léa was living two lives, divided by an invisible border she was obliged to cross and recross. By day, she was the cheerful girl the village had called its own since her earliest childhood. She visited the sick, lifting their spirits with her easy smile and frank, open laugh. She sterilized her father's instruments, sometimes standing by him shoulder to shoulder as her mother once had while he set a bone or stitched a cut. She taught children how to read and do sums, and she dreamed with aching impatience of a time when she could fashion her own future without regard for decrees or regulations or threats from men with guns.

By night, she followed the dark paths of war and tried to remember what it was like to be carefree. She did not think of herself as brave and was often tormented by nightmares of faceless men in black uniforms who had no ears to hear her screams. If she stopped to think about what she was doing, or what she had done, she wouldn't believe it.

She had to constantly adjust her frame of mind to the demands of the moment, but in the silence of her bedroom, she decided it was best not to think at all to avoid being immobilized by fear. It was in that silence that her love for her father and for Madeleine calmed her restless dreams and allowed her to maintain her sanity.

THE TWILIGHTS IN EARLY SEPTEMBER OF 1943 were so slow in their fading, it seemed as if the light would go on forever. The low sun cast gold on the stone of the *domaines*, and long, crazy shadows across the vineyards. But just two days before the harvest was set to begin, that dazzling light was snuffed out by a terrifying darkness.

The first sign of trouble was the silence. Colours seemed to drain out of the sky, leaving it an ominous and electric white. The air was suddenly heavy. Sensing danger, the blackbirds rose from the trees like plumes of smoke. The winds gusted, blowing sudden bursts of rain, first from one direction, then another. Then the clouds piled in, charcoal grey, deepening to black, ripped apart with jagged flashes of lightning that linked earth to sky.

Behind shuttered windows, Léa and all of Burgundy crouched in their homes and trembled at the violent wave of noise that followed. It was an indescribable yet unmistakable sound, a roaring that every vintner knew and feared in his bones. The hailstorm lasted for more than four minutes—rocks of ice flung haphazardly from the sky, tearing through vine leaves, pounding the grapes.

In less than half an hour, the sun was shining on a stunned landscape and the villagers gathered under the merciless sky to assess the damage done. Heads were hung and hands were wrung. More than one handkerchief was dug from a pocket to dab at disbelieving eyes. The low murmur of voices was punctuated now and then with a sharp French curse as the villagers waited for their scouts to report on the damage surely done.

The thick and twisted stems of plants that had survived for hundreds of years were snapped in half like toothpicks. The square was littered with torn leaves, shattered glass, and the broken bodies of songbirds smashed to the ground by the orbs of ice. Although it could not be true, Léa imagined the streets flowing red with the juice of the ruined grapes and the air was so dense with its smell, she could taste great mouthfuls of it whenever she drew a breath.

Soon scouts were returning from the neighbouring fields, reporting devastating news. Volnay, Pommard, and the southern *premiers crus* of Beaune were the hardest hit. Estimates placed the damage there at roughly seventy to eighty percent crop loss. In four minutes, an entire year's work had been wiped out. The storm had carried out its own cruel harvesting.

Across the square, Léa spotted Eugénie and ran to her, clasping her hands, but the gladness she felt at seeing her friend evaporated because Eugénie's hands were so cold, Léa could feel the chill from her fingertips all the way to her core. She feared that Eugénie was in shock, that the storm had been the last straw in a series of misfortunes that had sealed her unhappy fate. Léa looked around quickly for her father, but found Madeleine instead, her hands holding up her apron filled with birds that had been stunned and, with care, might fly again.

"Help me, Maddy. Eugénie needs to get warm."

"No, I'm fine," Eugénie protested. "My crop was spared. The lower slopes weren't hit. But the grapes are wet. They need to be picked as soon as possible."

Madeleine had removed her apron, tying it into a loose bundle that she'd set gently on the ground. She walked slowly towards Eugénie, who looked thinner and paler than when they had last met, and embraced her.

"I'll help you. My family will be there," Madeleine promised.

"And mine," added Dr. Legard.

"And mine," vowed Monsieur Drouhin.

And so it was that Léa watched the vintners who had suffered the most, whom she might have expected to be weeping with rage, instead step forward one by one to offer their help and their hands. The beauty of the gesture would sustain her for many months to come, and, at least temporarily, make the war irrelevant.

OUTSIDE, THE YARD GLITTERED WITH FROST and the last leaves of the chestnut trees rattled in the wind, a harsh, dry sound. It was the kind of late afternoon when winter darkness pressed up close to the windows and made a body glad to be snug inside, beside a fire, and in the company of a dear friend. Madeleine was brushing Léa's hair the way her own mother might have brushed it had she lived, smoothing down the long strands that felt like black silk under her hands.

"What do you wish for?" Madeleine asked.

Léa closed her eyes. She wished for so much—solace for her

father, reprieve from the German pestilence, and peace for her village, the return of Julien and the men who had disappeared into the Morvan—it was too much to ask and she was not bold enough to speak the words aloud and so carelessly tempt fate. If her wishes remained secret and unspoken, she could hold them close, nourish them with hope and prayer, and they might come true in some unfathomable way with the passage of time.

"I wish for a huge piece of that St. Honoré cake that your mother used to bake for Christmas Day and birthdays," she finally replied.

Both women laughed aloud because that cake, named for the patron saint of pastry bakers, was such a fantastic confection of puff pastry, whipped cream, and caramelized sugar that it was extravagant even in the best of times and beyond the power of the gods to fashion in wartime.

"Do you wish for love?" Madeleine continued.

"Who is there left to love? We're a nation of women and children now. Hens and baby chicks left to fend off the foxes."

"Then come and live with Eugénie and me. I'm going to move into the house because she's dying of loneliness. We can be three women, free and independent of men. At night we'll drink wine and talk of imaginary lovers who make no demands because they're perfectly absent."

But secretly, Léa did wish for love. When she was at church, she sometimes stole a glance at the statue of St. Agnès whose special gift was to help women find husbands. In times of war, the number of candles lit to honour the saint threatened to set her ablaze. Léa did not want the delirious passion of Madeleine's misadventure with Armand, nor did she need love in the desperate way that Simone did, as if to find a missing part, but her heart did wish for a certain kind of tenderness, for a face that would awaken an unknown pleasure in all her senses, a face that would be the last thing she saw before she died.

"I can't leave my father alone," was all she said. "Besides, isn't it risky—two women in a house without men?"

Immediately, Léa wished the words unsaid.

"Far riskier with men." Madeleine spoke lightly, but the strain that pinched her face for an instant told Léa that her friend was still coping with the trauma of Gaston's attack. "And, of course, we're not entirely alone. The dogs come into the courtyard at night."

"What dogs?"

"I think they come from the Morvan. Hungry dogs, some of them needing mending from bites, all of them needing love."

Léa shouldn't have been surprised. The same animals that she feared would tear her to bits whenever she entered the Morvan would kneel at Madeleine's feet. "But how ever do you feed them?"

"Mostly I can't. I sing to them. Every now and again the butcher gives me some bones too bare even for soup."

Léa could never find words exact enough to describe the sound Madeleine made when she sang to the animals. It had the metallic vibrato of a bell, yet the lightness and sweetness of a child's humming voice. Whenever animals heard that tender, undulating tone, they would sniff the air with curiosity and stretch their necks towards her. Léa felt it too. The sound just swept through her as if someone had opened a window and the breeze was lifting her hair.

Suddenly another, quite different sound caught Léa's attention and she held a finger to her lips to hush Madeleine who was still chattering about the sorry state of the dogs. Léa listened intently and heard again a light tapping at the window.

"Stay here, Maddy," she ordered, as she crossed the room and slipped out the front door. She was angry and afraid, ever mindful that a partisan found at her home could put her father's life in jeopardy because the Milice had never ceased suspecting that he was secretly aiding those dangerous saboteurs. But the slight figure standing on tiptoe to tap at her window was as unthreatening as could be imagined and shivering in the cold.

"Pierre, isn't it? Simone's nephew? What're you doing here? You'll catch your death in this chill. And why are you at the window instead of the door?"

"Aunt Augustine's nephew, not Simone's. Auntie's asked me to come, Mademoiselle. It's a secret. I didn't want anyone else to see me."

"Well, come through the front door now."

Pierre, all legs and arms in a thin coat and pants that were too small for his gangly limbs, stopped so abruptly when he spied Madeleine that Léa almost bumped into him.

"H-hello," he stammered.

"Pierre. What a surprise. How are you?" Madeleine smiled.

But the little boy could not manage a reply. He simply stared at her, a look of adoration on his not very clean face.

"Maddy, perhaps you could find something hot for Pierre to drink?" Léa tilted her head towards the kitchen and then guided the boy, whose eyes followed Madeleine's disappearing figure, into a chair.

"Now, tell me your secret Pierre. What does your aunt need from me?"

"She wants you to get a message to Gaston."

Léa could not have been more shocked had the child thrown a stone at her. Her pulse hammered at the base of her throat.

"I don't understand. Why does Augustine think I can help?"

Now it was Pierre's turn to look surprised. "Because you can contact the Resistance. Auntie thinks Gaston is with them, and there's a letter arrived from Simone, and Auntie says he can pick it up if he comes for food because the Germans at the house eat well and she can sneak some under their noses, only he shouldn't come to the courtyard this time, but tap at her window because the Germans don't pay any attention to old women."

Léa fought hard to keep her footing in this flood of words. "Listen to me, Pierre. Everything you've just said could get you shot. It could get your aunt shot, and me. I can't believe

Augustine could be so careless or so stupid. I won't help. You go back and tell your aunt I want nothing to do with any of this."

Pierre's face flushed and his lip quivered. "That's not fair. Auntie's not a traitor. Me neither. She's helped before and you know it."

"All right. I know she's helped. But this is dangerous. Do you understand how dangerous?"

"I'm not stupid. You don't know what careful is till you've got Germans living in the same house. That's why Auntie sent me. I can slip in and out. I can keep a secret. I didn't even tell Auntie that Gaston's not with the resistors."

Léa stared at the boy, and he stubbornly stared back.

"Do you know where Gaston is?" she finally asked.

"I'm not saying."

How long Madeleine had been listening, Léa could not guess, so riveted had she been on Pierre's revelations. She watched silently, every nerve in her body stretched, as Madeleine pressed a mug of milky coffee into Pierre's hands and knelt on the floor beside his chair.

"You can tell me," she murmured softly. "Won't you tell me where Gaston is?"

"I think he's in Pommard," Pierre blurted out, unable to resist the enchanted creature he believed Madeleine to be.

"Pommard? Do you mean he's working for Monsieur Benoir?"

"No, Mademoiselle. Madame Benoir."

"Madame Benoir? You must be confused."

The boy shook his head. "Gaston came to the house often."

"To visit Simone, surely."

"Simone in the evenings, Mademoiselle. Madame Benoir in the afternoons."

Madeleine's green eyes flashed with surprise, and she dared not risk even a glance in Léa's direction. "And why do you think Gaston is in Pommard?"

Pierre looked embarrassed. He ducked his head and began fiddling with the mug in his hands.

"It's all right. You're among friends. We can keep secrets, too," Madeleine promised.

"Well, I was bored. Simone was gone and the house felt so empty and I was just wandering around the halls and I couldn't help but hear them talking."

"And what did you hear?"

"At first, I thought they were fighting because I heard the bed hitting against the wall and Madame screamed like when she's having one of her tantrums, but then her voice got very soft and Gaston laughed. I didn't hear everything, but she said she'd pay him money to find someone in Pommard. She used a bad word, Mademoiselle. She said she'd pay money if he could find that bitch in Pommard. So, when Gaston disappeared, I figured he'd gone there."

Léa regained her senses before Madeleine could and broke the spell of Pierre's narrative, which was far more revealing than the child could know. "C'mon, Pierre. Time to get you safely home. I'll fetch a shawl to help keep you warm. Tell your aunt I'll send the message along. And don't worry. We'll keep your secret."

When Léa re-entered the room, Madeleine was still kneeling on the floor. She looked up at Léa and shook her head. "Poor Simone. All she ever wanted was to be loved. Imagine being betrayed by your own mother. Do you know who the woman in Pommard is?"

"No."

"Do you think Gaston is there?"

"No."

Madeleine looked away and stared into the fire. "No, I don't suppose he is, either."

DURING THE FOURTH WINTER OF THE OCCUPATION, the villagers of Volnay were sitting on a tinderbox of mutual hatred. They were struggling to breathe under the impossible weight of hostility, resentment, impatience, hunger, and the nasty smell of uniforms sweated and dried and sweated again. The villagers were sick of watery onion soup, mealy bread, stringy rabbit meat, and marching Germans who felt the need to make a point of their domination through showy processions of scissoring legs and heels beating hard against the earth. Madame Valleray declared that the marchers looked like angry toys, but no one was foolhardy enough to let the Germans hear any laughter at their expense because these were dangerous toys that might explode right in your hands and face.

In fact, the villagers were in more danger than ever because they were so exhausted from being constantly afraid that they were becoming numb and careless. Old men were just a step slower when told to move out of the way, the bartender's service in the café, a touch less snappy. At church, a head or two might turn toward the back pews where the three new members of the Benoir house sat, and the eye contact, assiduously avoided just a few months ago, would last a fraction too long.

Something inside the villagers was itching to be born, something alive and eager to be running free.

Of all the points of difference that marked a change in the villagers, it was this burgeoning spirit that the Germans could detect, even without their specially equipped vans that combed the countryside in search of invisible radio waves.

The situation worsened when March brought a clear blue ending to the winter and a reckless form of spring fever that was close to lunacy. Everyone knew the great invasion of the Allied forces was drawing near. Night after night, the BBC brazenly broadcast a flood of messages to resistance groups scattered across France:

Susie's hair ribbon is green.
Jack Porter has bought two new lambs.
The kittens have lost their mittens.
Eddie says hello to his cousin Mary.
The tomatoes are ripening on the vine.

The encoded messages taunted the sorcerers of the secret

police, inviting a series of wild speculations as they searched for patterns of meaning in this string of nonsense. *Green must mean go; ripening means the invasion is immanent; Jack Porter must be code for a harbour; everyone named Mary must be arrested immediately.* No one knew what to do about the kittens.

But somewhere in the vast darkness, someone understood the messages because never before had there been so many cut telephone wires or sabotaged railway lines.

In Volnay, clever and off-colour remarks were made about Yankee doodles, though very quietly. When one housewife visited another, it was a great joke to ask if the visitor wished for coffee or tea, as only the English would drink something as bland as that pale liquid made from crumbled leaves. One heady spring day, a man busy with the planting of new vines unconsciously whistled the opening bars of the *Marseillaise*.

The Germans, who kept impeccable records, noted every slight, every grudge and cold shoulder, misdirection, over-salted coffee, and inferior bottle of wine in their black ledgers. These villagers would pay for their folly and insolence. But while the villagers acted more or less spontaneously, bolstered by hope, the Germans, fuelled by an unspoken, unacknowledged, and dread fear of defeat, laid plans. The ruin that cruelty brings is always just a matter of time.

LÉA LOCKED THE SCHOOLROOM DOOR and turned towards home, eager for some quiet and some rest. The children were jittery these days, wriggling like puppies that had been penned in too long. They paid little attention to her, whispered behind her back, lost their place when they were reading, threw paper airplanes at each other, gazed dreamily out the windows, and generally made a nuisance of themselves. She did her best to be cross with them in an effort to control the chaos, but her heart wasn't in her scolding and the children knew it. The promise of summer and an Allied landing was too tantalizing, the reckoning of wrongs too near to be ignored. School days merely left

Léa exhausted, and the children triumphantly undisciplined.

As Léa crossed the village square, she was surprised to see Pierre waving to her. Like several other young boys, he did not come to school any longer, but helped in the vineyards because there were so few grown men to provide labour. Léa knew that Pierre spent hours at the Latour place, following Madeleine about like a hypnotized chick and presumably helping Eugénie.

"Mademoiselle Legard," he panted, as he ran toward her. "You must visit Madame Benoir. She told me this morning to catch you as you left the schoolroom."

Léa sighed and was about to refuse, but she was still alert enough to read Pierre's anxious expression. He was trying to catch his breath and his skin was slick with sweat.

"Have you run all the way from the Latours'?" she asked. She glanced around the square, spied a German soldier watching intently.

"Listen to me, Pierre," she whispered quickly, placing her hands on his shoulders. "You've missed school and you're afraid I'll be cross with you."

"What?"

She gave him a little shake. "Just play along," she hissed.

The shadow of the soldier fell across them. She felt Pierre's body stiffen.

"Good afternoon, Mademoiselle. Is there a problem?" The soldier's French was without accent and his voice genteel, but there was no doubt a person would do whatever it asked.

"No problem. I'm the school mistress, Léa Legard, as you probably know, and this boy has missed class."

"I do know who you are, Mademoiselle. I also know this boy. Pierre, isn't it? I thought you were working in the fields and exempt from class."

Was she imagining it, or was there a threatening tone in his voice?

"He still has lessons," Léa lied smoothly. "He does them in the evening and usually picks them up from me at the end of the school day. Today he was late, that's all."

The soldier raised his eyebrows, "I've never seen you with schoolbooks, Pierre."

Léa felt a stab of fear. She hadn't realized this man was one of the soldiers billeted at the Benoir house.

"I do my work in the kitchen," Pierre said. "Aunt Augustine will skin me alive and serve me to you for breakfast if I don't get home."

"I hope not," the soldier laughed. "Off with you then."

"Will you come with me, Mademoiselle?" Pierre turned and smiled up at Léa who had to admire his quick thinking. "Auntie will be pleased to see you and you can check my work."

"Of course." Léa slipped her arm through Pierre's and as they walked away from the soldier, she leaned her head towards him. "You're a clever boy. I think I've been underestimating you."

Pierre grinned. "You have to be on your toes all the time when you live with them. That's what Auntie says."

"Why does Madame Benoir want to see me?"

"I don't know. She trusts you. She says you're the only one who can help her."

"But I scarcely know her, Pierre. I've visited the house a couple of times. I've nodded to her at church. What does she think I can do?"

"Don't know, Mademoiselle. But whatever she wants, don't cross her."

They wound their way across the vineyards in silence, Pierre in the lead, Léa trying to bolster her confidence, trying to imagine what Madame Benoir could possibly ask of her. The house itself, with its Burgundian tiles, spacious courtyard, and expensive furniture, was intimidating, its mistress even more so.

Pierre took Léa into the living room and then scampered off. The carpet was from Asia in lush tones of purple and blue. The walls were covered with sheaths of blue silk wallpaper fashioned in Paris. Blue, thought Léa, was said to be the colour of loyalty, trust, and serenity, all qualities that Simone had confessed her mother was singularly lacking.

Madame Benoir was waiting for her, seated in a blue velvet chair. Her dark hair held a perfect wave that dipped across her forehead, and the dark red lipstick that traced the outline of her mouth enhanced the creamy skin of a flawless complexion. She neither stood nor smiled, simply waved Léa to a chair positioned directly across from her own.

The two women looked at each other without speaking. Léa was sure that Madame Benoir could read on her face every detail of the secret trysts with Gaston that Pierre had eavesdropped on, every small sigh, every moan of passion. Léa's confidence wilted under the scrutiny and she blurted out the first thing she could think of to break the silence. "How is Simone?"

"I haven't sent for you to talk about Simone. I want you to deliver a message to the camp in the Morvan."

A ripple of fear crossed Léa's face. How could this stranger know about the Morvan, or about her secret rides there on dark midnights?

"I don't—"

Madame Benoir raised a hand to interrupt her.

"There's no time for this. Do you know Hauptmann Karl Luders?"

Léa shook her head.

"He's an intelligence officer with so many secrets he's driven to confess some, just to relieve the pressure. Or maybe he was boasting. I'm not sure. It's difficult to tell with pillow talk."

"Pillow talk?"

"You needn't look so shocked. It wasn't that unpleasant. Hauptmann Luders has a great deal of stamina. The point is there's to be a raid in the Morvan. A traitor has given locations and names to the Gestapo. I don't know when, only that it will be soon. Maybe tonight, maybe tomorrow, maybe next week."

Léa stared into Madame Benoir's ice-blue eyes. Intuition told her that the woman was telling the truth. She wanted to hurl every insult she could think of at this woman for sleeping with the enemy, but she also wanted to thank her. Mostly, she wanted out of the room and away from the house where she could breathe fresh air. She stopped with her hand on the doorknob and looked back over her shoulder.

"Why? Why did you do it? You'll be the first person the Germans suspect should anything go wrong with their raid."

"My husband cheated on me with some whore in Pommard. My daughter is a thief. You didn't know that, did you? The worst kind of thief—the kind that lives in your own home. What would you do?"

"Not this," Léa said sadly. She tried to conjure up the depth of resentment and rage that could drive her into a Nazi's bed, but such a leap of the imagination was beyond her.

She was almost through the door when she heard Madame Benoir's last sentence.

"Maybe I did it to save Gaston."

Then you did it for nothing, Léa thought, and kept walking.

THE SITUATION WAS TOO GRAVE FOR LÉA to keep it to herself. She told her father everything. His face was ashen behind his black beard.

"My God, that woman could have half the village arrested. How does she know so much?"

"By sleeping with Gaston, I'd guess."

"He'd have done the village a favour if he'd vanished months earlier than he did. Who is this traitor?"

"She doesn't know or she chose not to say. Does it matter? I believe she was telling the truth about the raid. I must warn them."

"Out of the question. I'll go. I'll ride tonight. I know where the camp is."

The deserted caves were perfect for a guerrilla base: no logging roads led there, the approaches were well covered by rocks and dense tangles of underbrush, and it lay high enough that radio contact with London could be maintained on a more or less continual basis.

Léa grasped her father's hands. "No. Don't you see? I *don't* know where the camp is. One man will meet me. If I'm caught, if this *is* a trap, I can tell the Germans very little. But you, Papa, are their lifeline, and a dozen vintners would be willing to hide you in their wine cellars and keep you safe if I don't come back."

Dr. Legard's grip tightened on his daughter's hands. "You ask too much of me, Léa. This war asks too much. I forbid you to go."

"But Papa—"

"No. In fact, I don't even want you to be here tonight while I'm gone. Where's Madeleine?"

"She's at Eugénie's."

"Then go there. Go there now and stay there until you hear from me."

Léa tried tears, but her father was unmoved. "At least tell me when you'll ride," she whimpered, "so I can pray."

"The less you know, the better," he said firmly, but his stern demeanour melted when Léa threw her arms around him and he kissed her goodbye.

She started reluctantly down the road to the Latour vineyard, knowing her father was leaning in the doorway watching her every step, but when she reached the chapel next door to the vines, her stride lengthened and by the time she reached the courtyard, she was almost running.

Startled by her approach, Madeleine and Eugénie emerged from the stable, surrounded by five or six straggly dogs.

"I need your help," Léa panted.

"Of course," Eugénie replied, leading the way into the kitchen.

AT DUSK, THE FIELDS WERE SHADOWED in a purplish light, sunset faded to a few red streaks in the western sky.

Eugénie set off first, a small basket over her arm. She would reach the Legard home just as curfew fell, making it impossible for her, or Dr. Legard, to leave again without risk. The jar of jam in the basket was meant to sweeten the news of a disobedient daughter.

Clinging to Jacques' broad back, Madeleine and Léa and the dogs melted into the darkness. It would be a slow journey on the old plough horse, but the two women hoped their lack of haste would allow them to slip into the peacefulness of the night and so climb unnoticed to the protective covering of the trees on the high ridge behind the village. From there, they could reach the Morvan by midnight.

Jacques was not used to walking the forest paths, or lumbering over fallen trees and sidestepping puddles, but he carried faithfully on. When finally the edge of the Morvan loomed before them, absolute silence reigned. Madeleine and the animals found cover amid the mighty trees and Léa advanced alone.

For a moment, the rough landscape seemed enchanted. The breeze gently stirred the long grass and the treetops, and the frail light of the moon threw metallic rays across huge grey rocks in the distance. Léa had the illusion that she was in the dream of a sleepwalker where time had stopped and she was the only person on earth. She shook herself in an effort to wake up and whistled softly, but in the night's stillness, the sound was shrill in her ears.

She sank to the ground at the foot of a pine tree, exhausted from the tension of the ride. She listened and waited. She saw the brief silhouette of a hunting owl. Something rustled away from her across the floor of pine needles. Far above her, a cloud slid over the moon.

Finally, she heard the answering whistle of her contact and she rose to meet him, glad it was someone she knew this time— Henri, who had once sold vegetables in the village square and raided trains with Gaston.

They embraced briefly, then, heads almost touching, she told him everything she could about the raid and how she knew.

Léa considered it a good omen that Henri was on scout duty. Another man, a stranger, might not have believed her, but Henri had known her all his life and her words would convince him.

Her ordeal nearly over, she retraced her steps, almost running back to Madeleine.

"Halt."

The order was hurled into the air, so loud, so close, it seemed to shake the branches of the trees.

Léa instantly dropped to the ground.

Dazed and terrified, she heard the first vibrations of Madeleine's humming and, before her brain could fully realize what was happening, she saw Madeleine step calmly onto the forest path in full view of a trio of soldiers, pistols already drawn and aimed at the heart of that beautiful girl.

Léa felt like she was sliding down the sheer slope of a cliff, helpless, unable to halt the momentum of the scene Madeleine was intent on playing out not five feet from where she was hiding.

What Léa saw took her breath away.

Turning slowly at first, then twirling faster, Madeleine began to dance under an amazement of stars. Her skirt swirled around her, as she raised her arms to the sky. With her lithe figure stretched upwards and her tumbling mane of hair, she looked like a half-starved lioness, an exotic creature of the night, so beyond reason, expectation, and the soldiers' experience that they were transfixed. The pack of dogs bounded in circles around her, barking at the pale moon. Their eyes were cold and eerie, the enormous eyes of night animals.

No one could suppose this woman was real, so unbridled, yet so vulnerable that every soldier, if only for a moment, remembered some girl he'd once loved, and glimpsed in a flash the woman of his dreams.

Of course, as soon as the soldiers came to their senses, they arrested the mad woman and shot two of the dogs.

By the time Léa tumbled through her front door, Jacques'

mane was soaked with her tears and she was so distraught that her father merely picked her up and carried her to bed before Eugénie's dismayed eyes.

THE NEXT MORNING WAS A FRUSTRATING ONE for the Milice. The German soldiers had no intention of explaining to their own commander the intoxicating dance of a mad woman, so they dumped her at the feet of the local authorities. After the Milice had flung Madeleine like a weightless doll into a jail cell, they set about questioning the soldiers, but found them strangely tongue-tied and almost incomprehensible. Instead of giving a clear and no-nonsense account of where they had found Madeleine and what she had been doing, they kept going on about moonlight, dancing, and the eyes of dogs.

"She's a village problem. You deal with her," they finally muttered, and marched away.

Annoyed, the Milice dragged Madeleine from her cell, tying her to a chair so that she could not fail to be frightened by their complete control over her fate. Yet when they demanded to know what sinister plot against the state she was planning, Madeleine simply hummed. The men shouted at her and she smiled back. They yanked her hair and slapped her face, but she only stared at them from her green, sphinx eyes.

The only time she spoke was when they asked about the dogs and she urged her interrogators to adopt one each, because the abandoned animals were desperate creatures with sad eyes and only needed a dish, a kind word, and a piece of blanket to find happiness again.

The Milice were dumbfounded. Madeleine did not fit into any of the little boxes on the pages of their arrest forms. They didn't know what to do with her.

By noon, a small group, including the priest and Madame Valleray, had gathered outside the building. The Milice decided to invite the priest in and enlist the fear of god in their cause to break this stubborn woman. If the priest would threaten

Madeleine with excommunication and the voracious fires of hell, he might be able to convince her to be properly terrified and confess her sins.

This plan was defeated before it began because the priest merely crossed himself and assured the Milice that Madeleine had a scandalous past and was already a lost soul.

Finally, Madame Valleray elbowed her way forward.

"You'd best let her go," she insisted. "She's as mad as a box of frogs."

"Mad?" the leader of the Milice asked.

"Oh, yes," Madame Valleray testified. "Everyone knows. She talks to animals and climbs trees in the middle of the night."

There was an assenting murmur from the other witnesses.

At last there was a reason that would fit into the box of the bureaucratic form. The uniformed man wrote *Mad woman found after curfew with wild dogs* in a neat and precise script, signed the form with a flourish, and untied Madeleine.

Madame Valleray took her arm and led her away. Madeleine gave a sigh of relief and forgot all about the sordid surroundings of her imprisonment, the peeling walls, the cold metal bars, the smell of urine, the swelling of her cheeks where she'd been slapped, and even the claw of fear that had been lodged in her stomach for hours.

"I can't thank you enough," Madeleine whispered to her old enemy.

"Never mind, child. You may well be mad, but you're ours."

As she spoke, Madame Valleray swept her arm in an arc that took in the butcher, the baker, the café owner, the village square with its improbable fountain and snow white swans, the gentle slopes of green all around, and, high above, the benign face of Our Lady of the Vines shining down on them all.

IT BEGAN AS AN ORDINARY DAY IN EARLY MAY. An old cat, black, white and orange, was sleeping on a windowsill, opening one green eye now and then to study two boys in short pants kicking around a battered soccer ball. Madame Valleray was weeding her vegetable garden, dreaming of her son becoming Pope some day. Dr. Legard was writing up notes on his patients and Léa was trying to write a letter to Simone.

Dear Simone, she began. *Volnay is much the same and much less without you.*

Too sentimental. Also, not true. Most of the villagers scarcely noticed the absence of the spoiled girl from the big house.

Dear Simone, she began again. *Please stop writing to Gaston. He'll never answer you and I'm afraid you could stir up a lot of trouble.*

That at least was the truth, Léa thought, as she scrunched up the paper in her hand. She stared at the little bundle of letters from Paris, collected over the weeks from Augustine and Pierre. They were not lightly scented love notes, but angry little missives. The loops in the handwriting on the front of the envelopes were tight, as if a pen held in an angry fist had formed them. As she began and abandoned letter after letter to Simone, Léa realized that she could not invent a single story that would offer her friend the slightest consolation, and if, on the other hand, she told Simone the truth of all that she had learned, the blow would be terrible. As cowardly as it felt, Léa's only choice was silence.

The afternoon dragged by, unseasonably hot. Léa was almost asleep in her chair when she heard the first rumblings of the trucks. She ran to the window, calling for her father.

The two stood side by side, watching the Germans massing for an assault on the Morvan—at least fifteen platoons of soldiers with tracking dogs, machine guns, and field guns, passed by on the road. Léa's heart sank.

"The partisans will be slaughtered," she whispered.

"No. They'll be well hidden by now, thanks to your warning. They're much too smart to chance a direct confrontation. And they've known the paths of the Morvan since their childhood."

"I hope you're right, Papa," Léa replied, but she couldn't

shake her feeling of alarm. She prayed the Germans would not trace the warning back to Madame Benoir.

Later, she climbed to the high ridge behind the village and stared intently at the horizon. All she could see as dusk fell were showers of orange-red sparks, as if someone had lit a bonfire.

The village, she noted, as she made her way home, was unnaturally quiet, as if the whole community was holding its breath behind closed doors. The heat from the afternoon was trapped inside, making sleep, if it came, restless and crowded with unsettling dreams. The clock on Léa's bedside ticked slowly, measuring time in tortuous seconds.

She was jolted awake, came to her senses sitting upright in bed. *Get up*, she told herself, silently. *Right away. Now.*

She looked for her father first, but he was not in the house. She found Pierre, pale and frightened, banging at the front door.

"Hurry," he shouted, already turning away from her, racing across the fields.

Léa ran, following Pierre, asking no questions. The boy was quick and well ahead of her when she saw him stop and press himself, tight and small against the courtyard wall of the Benoir house. Léa crouched down beside him and peered through the bars of the courtyard gate.

An officer was barking orders, his face distorted and angry. Hauptmann Karl Luders, Léa supposed. As she watched, two men in overcoats came quickly out of the house, holding the arms of a woman.

It was Madame Benoir.

She was barefoot, though her feet barely touched the ground. She was wearing a blue silk nightgown, her hair was tousled and her eyes were shut. She stumbled and the two men jerked her upright and then pushed her into the back of a black car.

Léa grabbed Pierre and dragged him away. They reached the village square in time to see the black car drive slowly along the main road on the way to Gestapo headquarters in Pommard.

Villagers all along the way stopped whatever they were doing and watched, grim and silent witnesses. Though no one had bothered to really know her, or offer her true friendship, each of them understood too late that Madame Benoir had done something fine and brave for them or the Gestapo would not have arrested her. It mattered little that few among the witnesses knew exactly what Madame Benoir had done. They only needed to look at the face of Hauptmann Karl Luders. With his black, evil-looking eyebrows and hair stiff as a broom, it was easy to believe he was in league with the devil.

Such courage made Madame Benoir a saint of the war, and the villagers knew it. She needn't have lifted a finger, nor put herself in danger, but when the fateful challenge came to make a difference, she had walked out to meet it. Only Léa knew, instinctively and without a shadow of doubt, that Madame Benoir had also anticipated the inevitability of her arrest and had not expected to survive it. Once Luders' informant revealed that the Resistance had been warned of the raid on the Morvan, Luders would know the identity of the woman who had betrayed him.

By making the arrest public, the Gestapo sought to teach the villagers a sober lesson, but as the black car made its deliberately slow procession along the dusty road, a mad resolve blew through the village like a fierce wind. When the time came, this woman had taught them, they too would pick up their rabbit guns and their tools and fight back.

Léa heard a noise and saw that Pierre was crying, hiding his face in his hands.

Suddenly her father was beside her. He took Pierre's hand. "Your aunt is safe. But you can't go back. Come, live with us."

When the terrible day came to a close, and Léa finally climbed into bed, a sense of infinite loss rolled in from the night and filled her heart.

SIMONE AND HER FATHER RETURNED TO BURGUNDY two days later. They set up camp outside the Gestapo headquarters, but no one inside would talk to them or answer their pleas. It was rumoured that Monsieur Benoir's hair had turned white overnight, and only the fact that they were now living in Paris had saved both father and daughter from being arrested too. Finally, Dr. Legard found them on a cold afternoon when the sky was the colour of smoke, rescued them from their useless vigil, and brought them home.

As cruel as it seemed in the face of the Benoirs' shocked state, Léa and her father had agreed to say nothing about the true reason for Madame Benoir's arrest. They could do nothing for her, they'd decided, and though the Morvan was as silent as a mausoleum, without so much as a whisper about the fate of the raid, surely there were still others to protect. The only happy news they could offer was that Pierre and Augustine were safe at the Latour vineyard.

Monsieur Benoir looked like an old man Léa had never seen before. His shoulders slumped as he sat before the fire with misty eyes.

"It's my fault," he said again and again, like a sad incantation. "I should never have left her alone."

"No, Papa," Simone insisted, rubbing his shoulders and leaning close to his ear. "Maman chose to stay. She always was the one to choose."

Léa studied Simone from her corner of the room. Paris had been good for her, as though, when she'd left the village, she'd shed an old skin, or escaped like a bird let out of a cage, never to look back again. Her hair was shiny and her back was straight, but her hazel eyes darted around the room as if she couldn't fathom why or how the unpredictable winds of fate had blown her back to Volnay.

While Dr. Legard attended to Monsieur Benoir, Simone beckoned to Léa to join her in the kitchen, and her voice, when she spoke, was low and bitter. "We fought all the time, Maman and I. In the end, I gave up on her all together. When I was a child I wished that terrible things would happen to her, that she would fall down a well, or be kidnapped by bandits, or simply that she would leave us someday and never come back, but I didn't wish this upon her. What happened? What did she do?"

Léa shook her head. "No one knows for sure."

"Really? No one knows or no one will say?"

Léa glanced away from the stricken face of her friend. A mistake.

"You *do* know, Léa Legard. Why won't you tell me? Did she buy food on the black market, or insult an officer during one of her temper tantrums? Did she open up someone's private mail, or try to bribe someone? She was capable of any of that, you know. If you don't tell, my Papa will always blame himself."

Léa saw what was in Simone's eyes: confusion, anger, a desperate searching for an answer that would release her father, and maybe even herself, from the ruin of guilt. "I can't say much," Léa finally relented, "but your mother did something selfless. The villagers believe she discovered something that the Germans were planning and she warned someone, maybe even saved the village from reprisals. That's all I know."

"That's ridiculous," Simone sniffed. "That's not even remotely like the woman I know."

"Perhaps you didn't know her as well as you thought you did, perhaps none of us did."

"Who would she even care about in this wretched place? That old busy body, Madame Valleray? That pompous old priest who preaches gloom and doom?"

All Léa had to do was utter one name, *Gaston*. Utter that name and Simone might understand that her mother did care about someone, but it wasn't her daughter or even her husband. Some truths were just too brutal to tell. Léa turned away to leave the kitchen, but Simone's next question brought her to a halt.

"Where is Gaston? Is that also a secret no one is telling?"

For a moment, Léa feared that Simone could read her mind, that she could penetrate that small, dark place deep inside where she kept everything dangerous locked up. Just by thinking the name, she'd somehow released it into the open air. She'd hoped that if the name remained trapped in the limbo of unspoken words, it would eventually disappear. But here it was, again. Flapping about the kitchen like a black bird.

"Oh, Simone. I'm so sorry. Augustine gave me your letters. She thought I might be able to pass them on to the Resistance, but I didn't know how. "

There it was—a lie, an ugly toad fallen from her mouth to cover up an uglier lie. So serious did the moment feel to Léa that she couldn't believe Simone's reaction.

She was laughing. "The Resistance? Really? Does that sound like Gaston? Go ahead and burn the letters. When he does show up, I want nothing more to do with him."

BY MID-MAY, VOLNAY HAD NEVER SEEMED so beautiful. Birds, untroubled by the gravity of war, sang their hearts out and flocked to the trees in search of any cherries not already gathered up by the villagers, while the villagers smiled at each other with lips stained red with juice. Simone had coaxed her father to return to Paris where the family continued its efforts to find any trace of Madame Benoir, and in the soft evenings, Léa and her father bent their heads close to their clandestine radio and counted the odds for and against the Great Invasion that would soon, surely soon, sweep through the country.

In fact, Léa was so focused on the tantalizing promise of a new dawn that she forgot all about the urgencies of the night. When her father came to shake her awake, she felt disoriented and alarmed, without the invisible armour of alertness and quick thinking that had saved her in the past. When she stumbled down the stairs and into the living room, she had not the slightest premonition of the danger that awaited her.

There, panting for breath and bleeding profusely through a filthy bandage swaddled around his chest, was a partisan, his head cradled in Henri's arms.

"What are you doing here, Henri? Are you crazy?" Léa gasped.

No one answered her. Dr. Legard was already kneeling at the wounded man's side, and Henri glanced at her quickly with disappointment in his eyes.

But Léa couldn't stop herself. "Why didn't you wait and then bury him in the forest?"

Henri shook his head. "He wanted to see his mother before he died," he whispered.

Léa turned away then because she could not bear the way Henri was looking at her. She felt a hot flush of shame at her lack of pity. She climbed the stairs and dressed slowly and tried to clear her mind. When people grow up in a small village, she told herself, they learn all the best hiding places: the closet in the vestry of the church, behind the baker's flour sacks, between the narrow rows of vines. None of these would do. The vines were too open and the baker had no flour, and the priest couldn't be trusted.

She crept down the stairs and into the night. *When she was little and playing games with her father, she used to hide in the stable, but there was barely enough hay there now to feed her horse.* She slid from shadow to shadow, knocked softly at the window of a kind woman who used to feed her sweet biscuits from her apron pocket. *There was the trunk of her father's car mouldering away without gas, but it was sure to be searched.* She took the woman's hand and led her back to the Legard living room where the poor woman would face the worst moment of her blameless life.

Dr. Legard rose wearily and shook his head. Léa went to his side and guided him to the kitchen where they could still hear the muffled sobs of a mother, holding her son one last time as he died in her arms.

"You must leave now, Léa. It's too dangerous to stay. Go back with Henri."

"You're not coming with me?"

"We both know they'll be looking for us, expecting us to

be together. I'll hide in the wine *caves*, the interconnecting tunnels. The vintners trust me. But I don't know what to do with this poor boy. We can't leave him here for the Germans to find. His whole family will be shot. You and Henri must move quickly—you can't risk carrying the body back to the Morvan."

Léa took a deep breath and held her father's hand. "I know what to do with the body, Papa."

"What? What can we possibly do?"

She hugged him tightly and whispered in his ear. "Remember the night old Grenelle died and Gaston Latour disappeared?"

LATER THAT SAME NIGHT, Léa Legard mounted her horse and followed Henri to the Morvan, leaving behind her father and the village she loved. The wind unsettled her as it always had. It rushed over her smelling of restlessness, of a longing to be away, above the earth and part of the sky. She turned her face into the wind, opened her hands, and tried to cast away the feeling that something, somewhere was left unresolved, that some secret in the air around her was still waiting to be discovered.

EUGÉNIE

E UGÉNIE HAD ALWAYS LOVED living on the outer edge of the village, where a house could stand alone amid the fields, but still be connected, by tradition, by stories, and by thin roads to a network of other lives. The house stood tall and straight and even though the green paint had faded on the shutters and the downspout hung loose as a broken arm, it was still a home built by Eugénie's father for a woman to whom he had promised the world, or at least this lovely bit of it.

From her front door, Eugénie could see the stable, the court-yard with its table under the linden tree, and the green stripes of vines. She saw the vines as living things in need of care and loved how they grew, twisted and leaning toward each other like old friends. The grapes seemed not to notice the fragility of their source, and were firm and juicy and sweet. From her upstairs window, she could see the old, white chapel at the foot of Volnay, and while, by day, its stone was stained and crumbling, by night it shone like pale moonlight, illuminating the quiet earth where her parents now lay side by side.

Inside the house, the smells of her mother's cooking had seeped into the kitchen walls like wine into a tablecloth. Eugénie could close her eyes and almost taste the loaves of newly baked bread, a warm hunk in each hand for breakfast, or the roast chickens that sent the smell of lemons and rosemary slipping along the narrow lanes of the village, calling family and friends to the table. How many times had she sat as a little girl listening to the sounds of her mother—the rhythmic rap of her chopping knife, the clatter of spoons, the richness of her voice, loving, arguing, exclaiming aloud in laughter at some bit of village news that Eugénie's father brought through the door along with the smell of the earth and the sun?

She had an ocean of sky above her and a continent of trees in the forests around her, but the centre of Eugénie's world was that house and that vineyard. Her home was a nest built of memories and promises, even though she had accepted long ago that not every stick in the nest could be straight.

The first sharp pieces of the nest were the aunt and uncle that had come to look after her and her brothers, after the Spanish flu had felled her father like a tree, and had sapped her mother of strength until her bones and skin had been stretched pitifully thin. Aunt and Uncle were farmers from Toulouse, but not farmers of vines. The chalky soil had made them cross and they had not cared for the taste of wine. They were bitter that fate had interrupted their lives, demanding that they do their duty to the dead. As if that were not enough, there were these three bothersome children that needed to be fed and cleaned. Julien and Eugénie had watched Aunt and Uncle from the corners of rooms, communicating with each other in their silent language, and had grown up in spite of them. Everyone had been relieved when the twins turned eighteen. Aunt and Uncle had gathered up their suitcases and what cash they could and bolted.

Gaston had grown into a crooked straw, an unmannered and grasping child. Eugénie and Julien had tried their best, but he didn't seem to like any of the things they did. He was frightened of the horses when they'd tried to teach him to ride. When they'd played outside, he was always the one to be stung by a wasp or scrape his knee on a stone. His idea of pleasure was loading a slingshot with pebbles to torment birds, neighbours' cats, and boys at school. When he was punished, he would be sulky and nasty-tempered for days.

Eugénie thought he would grow out of his moodiness, but, in the end, he hadn't. He had just grown apart from her, disconnected himself from the nest, and by the time the malignant shadow of war crept over the land and Julien rode away, she really didn't know her little brother anymore, and much of what she did know of his wildness alarmed her.

Alone, Eugénie was often lost in the realm of nostalgia, where events shifted, slid, and changed, and where one memory flowed through her and then another, as effortlessly as one wave following another.

There she was at six years old, throwing thin, flat stones across the surface of a lake in the Morvan, watching them sink and disappear while Julien's rocks skimmed, dipping, and then spinning up like wild birds.

"You'll kill the fish that way," he laughed, as her latest stone hit the water with a heavy splash and sank.

"Show me?" she asked.

And he put a new stone in her hand, tilted her wrist, taught her how to fling the stone sideways until finally one spinned, dancing on the water like the light from the sun, like the light in Julien's eyes. He was her net, always there to catch her, midfall. The pain of being separated from him was like the pain the injured claim to feel in a phantom limb.

There she was again at ten years old, with Gaston in her arms, his body pounded by sobs, her lips on his hair, whispering that Mama and Papa had loved him so much, that she was sorry, that she was there and always would be there, while he shook as if crying were a new kind of breathing until finally he slowed and she held him, quiet, through the end of the day, while the noises of doctors and neighbours and condolences rose and fell around them.

But at some point, Eugénie had opened her arms, unclasped her hands, looked away—she didn't know how or when—and Gaston had slipped through her fingers. Their relationship became a series of doors slamming, arguments simmering, erupting, and then disappearing into bitter silences. While Eugénie struggled to save the vineyard, her signature upon the earth, she knew from the way Gaston looked at her that he felt nothing for her and her life's work but resentment, and perhaps even contempt.

She also knew, for reasons she couldn't fathom, that part of that resentment extended to Madeleine Vernoux. His eyes glittered when he looked at her and her simple presence seemed to provoke him, as if she represented something else he couldn't have.

"Leave her alone. Please, Gaston," Eugénie pleaded, but he just stared at her with a shuttered expression and pushed her harshly aside.

Eventually, the desire to go grew so big in Gaston, filled him so much, that he always seemed to be in a rush, as if to catch the last train to somewhere more important. He told her he was going to Paris, going to leave the vineyard forever, that he didn't care if he ever saw it, or her, again.

"I'm going into the village now," she replied, without even the pretence of asking him to stay.

WHEN EUGÉNIE RETURNED HOME that August afternoon, the low sun shone in a golden slant across the vineyard. She propped her bicycle against the wall of the house and began to gather up her meagre purchases, but something stayed her hands, some premonition tugged at the edges of her consciousness the way Gaston used to tug at her skirts.

She pushed the memory away. She mustn't think of him any longer as he once was, a little boy needing her. He didn't need her anymore, didn't need the land or the comfort it could offer, or the love she once held out to him that had curdled over the years.

She lifted her head and surveyed all that she knew so well, the way the breeze played with the leaves of the linden tree at this time of day, where the shadows lay, the dusty green smell of sage from her herb garden. Her eyes fastened on the single detail that didn't fit. The stable door was unlatched.

It was such a simple detail with a dozen banal explanations—perhaps Madeleine had forgotten to secure the door, or perhaps she was still inside, fussing over Jacques, or perhaps the latch was broken—but for reasons Eugénie would never be able to explain, her hands began to tremble.

She walked slowly to the stable door and swung it open. She took one step, and felt the snap of a shard of glass beneath her foot. Wide-eyed, she saw the pale green wine bottle smashed to pieces and spattered with blood. Shadows fanned across the floor of the stable, deepening, stretching toward her, engulfing her finally. She heard a sound, a soft moaning sliding up several octaves until it became a jagged cry, but whether it was torn from her own body or from the darkness descending upon her, she could never say. Her mind was empty, a blank, a weak flame that guttered and went out.

MUCH LATER, EUGÉNIE WOKE with a start, and a sense of rising panic. She was in a place she'd never been before, though she lay in the bedroom she'd known all her life. Outside, in the night, she heard a tawny-owl calling. She thought of the night outside, the owl's searching flight. The dark stable. Something terrible had happened in the stable. A shrieking. A field mouse maybe in the rough grass between her home and the white chapel, the owl's prey. There was something she should be doing, something to do with the owl's flight or bats on the wing—it wasn't too late in the year for bats. She wasn't finished yet. Julien would know what to do. But Julien wasn't here. She felt that everything was made of glass, glass in the stable. Love was like glass. At first, it was so clear you opened your hands to reach for it, only to have the glass cut you, leaving you to watch blood running through your fingers, splashing uselessly to the ground. She thought maybe there were bats in the stable, or maybe there was something on the ground. She wondered why her limbs were so weak and sluggish and her ideas so jumbled, but fell into a deep sleep before she could work out an answer.

August 26, 1943

Dear Julien,
We played in streams and rivers. We swam in ponds.
The old folk say water has a perfect memory and is always trying to return to where it was. Perhaps you will, too. Remember the water. Follow the banks of the river Saône and swim home to me.
Love,
Eugénie

Over the next few weeks, she knew the villagers were asking questions about Gaston, which was why she walked around with knots in her stomach, and why her hands shook. Then the soldiers came pounding through her house, their big German voices banging into her. She stood still, gripping the back of a chair, while they ransacked the stable, knocked down furniture, ripped open mattresses, kicked at the walls and shouted at her. She was sure she would be executed on the spot, but the soldiers didn't find a thing and finally left, kicking the door one last time to express their frustration.

After a month or so, and no word, no news, the churning in her stomach was replaced by a more certain and deeper ache. It seemed a thing beyond belief, but Gaston was nowhere to be found, least of all by her. She walked through her days in a daze, barely able to comprehend that both of her brothers were gone.

The inside of her head sounded like wind rushing by. She reached for things and couldn't feel them. It was as though everything solid had slipped away. She was tormented by everyday incidents that suddenly seemed like pointed metaphors of disappearance: water vanishing into steam as the kettle boiled, salt dissolving in water, mist evaporating in the dawn's warmth, clouds blocking the moon's glow, raindrops sinking into the thirsty soil, scents dissipating into thin air.

She noticed that people were avoiding her, as if she were giving off sparks of distress. Eugénie understood that it was important to hide her deepest self. People couldn't live in a village like Volnay and do whatever they liked and say whatever they felt. The world would tilt if she wept openly in the village square. There had to be rules and secrets.

Everyone wanted the old Eugénie, the somewhat plain, hard-working, tall girl with smoky black hair and a crooked smile, and a deep, quiet centre like the taste of a good red wine.

But that Eugénie had been swept away by grief and regret, as if by a river in flood. Its powerful torrents altered the landscape so that nothing she saw looked familiar any longer. It seeped up insidiously from under the floorboards of her house so that soon she was not walking, but wading in cold water. At night, in dreams, its currents sucked her under, leaving her gasping for air. The new Eugénie struggled to stay afloat, and she knew that the moment she gave up, she would sink like a stone.

She tried to anchor herself in the vineyard. She loved the mineral smell of the earth after the rain, the feel of the soil crumbling in her hands. Her father had once told her that whatever the wind did not blow from the earth settled in and dug deep.

Eugénie settled in and was not moved by the winds of change. Over time, her schoolmates had travelled to cities like Paris or Lyon, or taken jobs in the village, or married the boys they loved. But Eugénie remained tethered to the earth, waiting by the window for Julien to come home. Now she feared that the vineyard would never survive, that the pane of glass would become her world, and the empty road her fate. Her fierce single-mindedness had surely turned Gaston against her and she, alone, must shoulder the loss and the blame.

When the windows were shut and the curtains were drawn because she could not bear to keep seeing the empty road, she was sure she could smell the essence of Gaston trapped inside the house, the smell of Gitanes and red wine, sweat and something sour like curdled milk. She knew it was impossible, but the invisible odour was everywhere, in the curtains and furniture, in the kitchen, and even in the pockets of her clothes. She found herself looking for him behind doors and in closets, once even kneeling to peer under his bed.

She began to fear laying eyes on a phantom Gaston who would surely haunt her and drive her slowly mad, and be pleased to see her plunge into emotional chaos. She knew the ghost was present when her heart beat too fast. He was like a dark shadow gliding everywhere, crossing her line of vision and then fading away. She felt the phantom following her everywhere, next to her in the queues for bread, beside her in church, and she wondered that other people didn't stare or run away in fright.

At night, Eugénie's sleep was torn by nightmares and, as the summer slipped away and the harvest beckoned, she felt increasingly unsteady and exhausted, as if her fear of ghosts had eaten away her muscle and softened her bones. The lack of sleep seemed to make time mutable. Entire days went by sometimes without her noticing. One morning, she refused to get up or open the blackout curtains. She had begun to take leave even of the light, and enter slowly into darkness.

So when the hailstones began to crash down to earth from the sky in a thunderous roar, it was as if the land itself were shaking Eugénie awake, forcing her to get up, to act, to feel, to be. She ran into the vines and flung herself onto the ground, listening for the faint pulse of the earth. Rain soaked her hair and drenched her clothes, but no ice ripped through the leaves of her vines. Her field had been spared that pounding.

She stumbled into the village and saw the devastation of the upper slopes of Burgundy written on the grim faces of her neighbours. She saw them step forward one by one to help her, their kindness flooding her heart and leaving her open-mouthed with gratitude. All that day and into the night, she worked shoulder-to-shoulder with the villagers harvesting her grapes, leaving not even the smallest space into which a ghost might slip. When the work was done, and Jacques had pulled the wagon of grapes to the local co-operative, she knew that her year's work had been saved and a new season on the land had begun.

MADELEINE'S DECISION TO STAY ON at the farmhouse was a bridge leading Eugénie back to life. The two friends suffered one awkward and charged exchange when they first spoke of Gaston to each other. Madeleine reached for Eugénie's hand. "I'm sorry about Gaston," she said simply.

"Me, too," Eugénie replied. She hesitated, stretching out the silence. She might have said more, might have asked questions or shared secrets, but the still look in Madeleine's eyes stopped her and the tantalizing moment passed.

Madeleine could not fail to notice the decline of Eugénie's spirits in the sorry condition of the farmhouse. Dust and cobwebs had collected in its dark corners. Flowers had wilted in their vases, saturating the air with their musty, lingering odour. The leaves of plants had withered and fallen off because no one had bothered to water them. Mice had invaded the kitchen where uneaten bits of food had congealed on unwashed plates.

As she had once before, Madeleine swept through the entire house like a fresh breeze. She shooed the mice away, polished every surface until it gleamed, and even painted the walls a bright yellow so that the sun would always shine inside and banish every shadow. She coaxed the doves to nest on the windowsills, so that when Eugénie came to stare at the empty road, the birds would fly up and fill the panes with flapping wings.

"Let Julien surprise you," Madeleine urged. "It's better if you don't see the future coming."

The only place in the farmhouse left intact was Gaston's bedroom. Eugénie kept the door locked. She didn't want anybody going in there, and she especially didn't want Gaston's spirit coming out.

Madeleine waved that superstition away with a flick of the wrist, but decided to respect Eugénie's wishes because any sleep to be had in Gaston's lair would surely be contaminated by nightmares. She moved into Julien's bedroom instead, keeping his photo on a small table and looking into his kind eyes and angular face every night before she put out the light.

During the fall, the two women raked the leaves into bonfires, as if raking away the summer itself, and during the winter, they knit warm scarves and socks for the parcels they hoped would reach Julien in his prison camp. Eugénie explained that the camp in Silesia was for officers who were entitled to *tickets colis*, labels the French prisoners of war were issued to obtain food and other provisions from home. They were like shipping permits, and each POW was given one label a month to send home. No package sent back could weigh more than five kilos, and it had to have the label attached.

"Of course," Eugénie added, "there's never any guarantee the Germans will deliver them, and even when they do, the packages have always been opened and pilfered. I tried to send a book once because Julien loves to read, but I don't think he got it. Mind-numbing boredom is his worst enemy, but hunger is a close second. At the beginning of the war, I sent him three eggs packed in flour so they wouldn't break, but now there's not enough flour."

Madeleine was both horrified and inspired by this story. Over time, her menagerie had settled into the courtyard, a collection of motley dogs, abandoned cats, once pampered and now returning to their feral prowls, Jacques the gentle giant, and birds with iridescent necks and dashes of red at their wingtips that flittered in and out of the stable. She began to follow the birds everywhere, picking up feathers whenever they drifted by and visiting the swans in the village pond regularly. When finally she had enough feathers to fill a box, she presented her prize to Eugénie.

"Now you just have to find the eggs," she laughed.

The next day, Madeleine pulled two eggs from the pocket of her coat, presented them to Eugénie and put a finger to her lips. "Stolen by little Pierre from the Germans staying at the Benoir house," she whispered.

The grinding boredom of Julien's prison camp was a more difficult problem to solve. Eugénie wrote almost every day to her brother, but she received so few letters in reply, and even those censured, that she had to assume her own mail seldom reached him. She wished she could write out one of the outlandish stories that Madeleine told on long winter nights, but there wasn't enough paper and she was sure the Germans would seize it in any case for its subversions of reality. Madeleine's stories were always happy ones because, as she put it, Eugénie was a magnet for tragic twists of fate and only a steady diet of the miraculous could cure her.

"We could write the story in code," Madeleine suggested, "one line per letter. That way, while he waits for the next instalment, he can imagine all the different paths the story might take."

Eugénie loved this idea because she and Julien had shared a secret language when they were children, a simple code in which every fifth word was significant. While Madeleine sat at the kitchen table to conjure up an impossible heroine with green mermaid hair and honeyed eyes, Eugénie scoured the farmhouse for scraps of paper, even using the inside of the wrappings of a bar of soap or a bouillon cube. When the letter was finally ready to send, the two friends were sure that its flawed syntax and odd vocabulary would entertain Julien for hours, or, at the very least, keep the German guards scratching their heads trying to decipher it.

November 14, 1943
Dear Julien,
The harvesting is done. There was a terrible hail-
storm, was. We were spared though, once. Madeleine
Vernoux has come, a friend to stay, a woman. Every
night she sleeps with your picture in a green nightgown.
She tells stories, mermaid stories. She has beautiful hair.
We're sending you jam and wish it could be honeyed
wine. I miss your eyes.
What happens next?
Always,
Eugénie

ON SOME NIGHTS, MADELEINE'S PARENTS would come to visit
and Eugénie would drag out the old phonograph and put on
a jazz record. The foursome would sit by the fire while the
sad, sensual moan of a saxophone and the low, deep voice of
a woman in love flowed around them. If the music were too
heart-wrenching, however, the dogs in the courtyard would
begin to howl and Madeleine would be sent out to calm them
down by singing to them, her voice trilling like an enchanted
flute. Madame Vernoux's favourite song was the 1938 melancholy hit "J'attendrai" by Jean Sublon, but Madeleine forbade
it as too poignant a reminder of Eugénie's frequent trips to the
window where she waited for the first signs of Julien's return.

Spring was already in the trees when Eugénie and Madeleine
were reminded by Papa Vernoux that the war was moving
ahead in leaps and bounds, in directions the Germans were
no longer able to control. "Be careful," Papa warned. "This
is not a time to be reckless. The ranks of the Resistance are
swelling and each time a train blows up, I fear the Germans
will take revenge on the village."

The next time Eugénie went to market, she saw for herself
that the faces of the soldiers in Volnay were marked with the
lean contours of hunting dogs.

Still, neither woman hesitated when Léa Legard appeared in the courtyard with a plan to warn the partisans in the Morvan of the Germans' impending raid. Eugénie's part was small— hers was the unenviable task of telling the good doctor that his daughter had deceived him and was riding into danger—but it was a night Eugénie would never forget.

She sat in Dr. Legard's living room with her hands folded on her lap, feeling the burn of treachery in her mouth.

"Why didn't you stop her, Eugénie?" he demanded. "You're the sensible one."

But Eugénie knew she wasn't sensible. She hardly knew who she was anymore. Despite Madeleine's intervention, she still suffered terrible headaches that shattered into pieces and cut into her temples. She suffered from nightmares and saw ghosts. There was no one with whom she could speak about these things, not even the doctor, because people preferred not to know. She felt incapable of sustaining her hope that Julien would ever return or that she would ever be able to explain to him about Gaston. It was only Madeleine, with her natural gaiety and capacity for tenderness, who kept her upright and functioning.

"She seemed determined to go, sir," was all she could say, and the doctor had thrown his hands in the air as if to emphasize how inadequate a response that was, and how much she had disappointed him.

Eugénie felt false to the very core of her being. She watched the doctor pace the floor and listened to the cruel ticking of the clock, and knew she could do nothing to ease his anxiety. Who was she, after all? A simple village girl who worked in the vineyard, the orphaned keeper of a lost cause. She'd done nothing to help win the war, had saved no one. She felt invisible and ineffectual. When Léa stumbled through the door, distraught, and without Madeleine, Eugénie thought she might vanish altogether in a puff of smoke.

Eugénie wanted to rush into the street to look for Madeleine, but Dr. Legard said they must wait, that no one must know they were even aware of Madeleine's capture. He left her alone with her promise to stay put and went to sit by his daughter's bedside.

The darkness in the room was complete. Eugénie stared into it almost without blinking. It was the darkness of a bat's wing, the darkness of the stable, the darkness of a soul. The hours ticked by like the countdown of a timing mechanism rigged to a bomb.

Sometime near the blue mists of dawn, Eugénie finally surrendered her hope that Julien would ever return, in order to go on living. She simply let go, took a deep breath and felt an uprooting in her heart, like the uprooting of an unhealthy plant. Her relentless hope, that had so estranged her from Gaston, had become a kind of imprisonment, an endless, exhausting anticipation that prevented her from living in the present and trapped her in the past. Another woman waiting: what use was that? She was merely a buzzing fly, banging into a pane of glass over and over. Enough. If Madeleine were still alive, Eugénie wanted to be alive too. She could not waste her life searching for Julien's face.

When Madeleine walked through the door at noon, Léa rushed down the stairs and threw her arms around her, but Madeleine looked directly at Eugénie, saw the lightness that comes from releasing a burden of the heart, and smiled.

SHORTLY AFTER THAT UNFORGETTABLE NIGHT, Madame Benoir was driven away in a black car, and Dr. Legard brought Augustine and Pierre to stay in the farmhouse. No one knew what the Gestapo would do next and no one in the village ventured out while the soldiers roamed the streets like the lost wolves of Burgundy howling in the darkness of the curfew.

Pierre was especially terrified for he had witnessed the brutality of Madame Benoir's arrest: the screeching of brakes, the slam of a door, the crush of boots, a scream cut off in mid-pitch. He had heard the great house pant with the laboured breath of a beaten woman. So pressing was the child's need, that Eugénie unlocked the door to Gaston's room without a moment's hesitation. She flung open the window and stripped the bed, without smelling anything or seeing a single apparition. She wrapped Pierre up in her own blankets and held his hand, while Madeleine sang to him until he fell asleep.

Augustine sat in the kitchen with her elbows on the table, muttering the curses of a sailor. Her old bones ached as much as her heart. "She could be selfish and more stubborn than a mule," Augustine revealed, "but Madame loved that man."

Eugénie supposed Augustine was referring to Monsieur Benoir, but Madeleine urged the old woman to come to bed and changed the subject of the conversation.

THE SUN OF LATE MAY CALLED EUGÉNIE BACK to the land and she was happy to obey. Her days began at dawn and lasted until the vivid haze of sunset. She felt an almost mystical connection to the vines and allowed them to set the rhythm and pace of life. While Augustine took control of the shopping and the cooking, Madeleine and Pierre helped Eugénie with the vines—pruning, checking for maladies, tying back shoots that had come loose.

Pierre quickly recovered from the shock of Madame Benoir's arrest and was full of questions. "Why don't we just water the vines?" he asked when Eugénie searched the sky for signs of rain.

"Irrigation is forbidden," she replied. "We want the vines to dig deep into the soil."

"How deep?"

"Four or five metres so the wine will hold all the flavours of the deepest earth."

Eugénie had grown up with all the myths and legends of wine-growing, traditions that in many ways had changed little since the Middle Ages. She told him that plowing, pruning, and picking were once done according to the phases of the moon;

she told him that St. Martin's donkey had once chewed the leaves of a vine right down to the trunk, and the monks were surprised when that same vine was the one that grew back most abundantly and produced the best grapes, and that was how the *vignerons* learned about the virtues of pruning. And she amazed him when she told him that naked men were once plunged into the frothy liquid of the crushed grapes in order to stir the must with their entire bodies.

"You mean they swam in the grapes?" Pierre asked.

"Not exactly. They held tightly to chains fixed to overhead beams and raised and lowered themselves in the liquid. If they lost their grip, they could drown or be asphyxiated by the carbonic gas given off by the fermenting juice."

When Madeleine heard these stories, she shook her head and believed that her friend's tales were becoming as fanciful as her own, and Eugénie agreed because, when day after day passed in the same way, time became almost magical and it felt never-ending.

But, of course, it did end in a brutal fashion when Augustine, dressed in her customary black, appeared in the field like the witch of fairy tales filled with bad tidings, bringing the ominous news that Léa Legard and her father were missing and their house was completely empty, with the door left ajar and blood on the living room floor.

As the hours crawled by and no good news came to calm their fears, Madeleine grew frantic. Eugénie did her best to bring her to her senses and understand how dangerous it would be to go searching for Léa or ask questions that would alert the prowling Gestapo. Augustine stood to the side, watching what was quickly becoming a battle that Eugénie was losing, and wisely dispatched Pierre to fetch Madeleine's papa.

He came with a rope hidden behind his back and recognized instantly the first signs of the mania that had seized Madeleine when Armand Valleray had forsaken their tumultuous love affair.

"I forbid you to go anywhere, Daughter," he shouted, flourishing the rope. "If you force me, I'll tie you to a chair."

Madeleine was so shocked by the threats of her father, who had never before raised his voice against her, that she felt the fight flow out of her like an ebbing tide. An alert Augustine seized upon the opportunity to coax Madeleine to drink a glass, and then another, of fortified wine—already strong, but made even stronger by a concoction of chamomile and valerian root that she had brewed in the kitchen while Eugénie was wasting her breath with mere words.

Within a half an hour, Madeleine's beautiful head was nodding, and her papa carried her to her bed where she fell into a deep sleep.

"What will we do with her in the morning?" Eugénie asked.

Papa handed her the rope. "In the meantime, I'll see if I can find out what's happened."

There had been no Gestapo crashing through the Legard's door, Papa was able to report later. Léa's horse was not in the stable, nor the doctor's bag in his study. Most of the villagers, who knew for a fact that the doctor had been treating the partisans since the beginning of the Occupation, assumed the time had simply come for the Legards to go into hiding.

"That's right," Augustine nodded. "Léa will have gone to the Morvan where Henri will ride alongside her. And the doctor has plenty of friends who'll gladly hide him in the tunnels of their *caves*. Gaston took me there once. There's a multi-layered labyrinth underground that the Germans know nothing about, and would surely get lost in if they did. You can enter one tunnel in a field near Pommard and come out on a street in Beaune."

Eugénie regarded Augustine as if she were seeing her for the first time. She'd known nothing of her relationship with Gaston, and nothing of her involvement with the Resistance. In fact, she had to admit that she had preferred not to know anything about the Resistance in order to maintain her precarious stability in a world that was crumbling beneath her feet. She had been purposely blind. It was then that she understood that the days of Nazis were numbered because they would never be able to crush the spirit of Augustine, or prevent the many small and unheralded acts of bravery of ordinary, common sense women like her, who surely must exist all over France in every city and village.

When Papa Vernoux was satisfied that Madeleine would sleep for some time and be placated by the fact that Léa was still free, he took his rope and went home.

Eugénie poured two glasses of wine and lifted hers in a toast to Augustine. "How can I help?" she asked.

"We'll see," was the reply.

BY CHANCE, EUGÉNIE WAS THE ONLY ONE in the household still awake when Léa came tapping at the window two midnights later. She had been poring over her financial books trying to find a way to stretch her resources even further when she heard the dogs begin to growl and caught a glimpse of a face staring in at her from the night outside. At first, she thought it was a ghost and her heart sank to think the haunting shadows had returned to torment her.

But in the blink of an eye, Eugénie saw that this was a face she was glad to welcome and she ran to the door.

"Help us," Léa whispered, motioning with her arms in the direction of the stable.

Eugénie hesitated. The stable made her uneasy. It slammed into a black space inside her head, and she rarely ventured into it, especially now that she had Madeleine to care for Jacques. But she stepped out into the night, quieted the dogs, crossed the courtyard, and stood in the doorway.

Henri held the reins of two horses. Léa knelt in the glow of a small lantern, and Eugénie saw a man with a smashed leg lying on the ground. His head and the upper part of his face were completely covered in bandages, and his mouth in the midst of a reddish-coloured beard was grimaced in pain.

"Please," Léa said. "We can't care for him and I don't know where to find my father. Will you take him in? I know Augustine would help."

"Not here," Eugénie replied. "Can you move him?"

She saw the light dim in Léa's eyes at her refusal and stepped forward quickly. "I only mean not here in the stable. If he can be moved, I have another place to hide him where he'll be safer."

Léa and Henri nodded, shouldering the weight of the man between them and Eugénie walked into the vines to the shed with its underground *cave* where Gaston had once stashed the contraband goods he had stolen from the German trains.

"I wish there were still some food here," Eugénie said, "but it's all gone. At least there's a blanket."

Léa and Henri manoeuvred the man down the stairs and tried to make him comfortable.

"What happened to him?" Eugénie asked.

"He was coming in on a Lysander," Henri explained, while Léa tried to swaddle the man in the blanket. "It clipped a tree and crashed."

"A Lysander?"

"A light plane, just room enough for two. The pilot didn't make it."

When Léa was satisfied she had done all she could, the three solemn figures walked back to the courtyard.

Léa took Eugénie's hand. "I'm sorry, Eugénie. I should have told you he's an agent, but I see now that it wouldn't have made a difference. In any case, it won't be for long. Give Madeleine a kiss for me."

Eugénie stood alone until the sound of the horses faded away into nothingness. The nameless man was an agent, which meant that if the Germans found him, he and the entire household would be shot or, at best, deported. She suddenly had a lot of lives to protect.

THE NEXT MORNING, EUGÉNIE CALLED everyone into the kitchen and confessed that she had helped to hide the nameless man in the *cave*. "You've a right to know," she said solemnly, "because all our lives are at stake. He's an agent. If he is found here, we are lost."

"Where's he from?"

"How is Léa?"

"How badly is the man hurt?"

The questions from Pierre, Madeleine, and Augustine crowded around Eugénie, but she had few answers.

"Léa was fine and with Henri. They rode horses. All I know is that she said it wouldn't be for long."

"Why?" asked Madeleine.

"I'm not sure. But she said she couldn't find her father and the man clearly needs doctoring. Perhaps she meant he'll likely die."

"Too risky to bring Dr. Legard out of hiding," Augustine insisted. "There's posters up in the village now, with a fat reward for anyone who can turn either him or Léa over to the Gestapo. We'll have to fix up this man ourselves."

"Whatever you've been feeding me over the last few days will surely knock him out," Madeleine grinned. "At least he needn't be in pain."

The four sat together for an hour or so, making plans and trying to strategize the best way to minimize any neighbours' suspicions. Eugénie would be the only visitor to the *cave*. People were used to seeing her go in and out because she kept her tools there and was so often in the fields. Augustine would brew whatever combination of herbs might ease the man's pains, and Madeleine's dogs would continue to be their best warning of any approach by soldiers. Meanwhile, Pierre would try to beg or steal extra food, because he had the natural cover of always being hungry himself, and because he had already established himself as an inventive thief. Madeleine would visit her parents for any news leaking from the BBC, and, if there were any need to venture out after curfew, well, the village was used to seeing Madeleine trespass through the vines under the stars.

It was noon when Eugénie approached the *cave* with a bottle of doctored wine, a heel of bread and an extra blanket hidden in her wheelbarrow. Sometime during the morning, it had rained. The skies had opened and washed the fields, leaving the air bright and clean, smelling of greenness and moisture.

She raised the trap door and descended the stairs as quietly as she could, not knowing if the man was sleeping and fearing that he might already be a corpse.

"Who's there?" The voice was raspy, but the words were in French.

"I'm Eugénie," she said, kneeling beside the injured figure. She lifted the blanket and looked at his leg, saw that Léa had used pieces of wood to fashion a splint. Even the slight movement of the blanket seemed to cause him excruciating pain, but Eugénie could not see any signs of infection.

She studied the lower half of the face, pale as wax, which was all she could see because of the bandages around his eyes and forehead.

"Who are you?" she asked softly. "Where are you from?"

She watched his lips tighten into a thin line, a refusal to respond, and realized how disoriented he must be, a bird flung out of the sky, blinded by pain. The odour of pine trees, smoke, and dried blood breathed from his skin. She reached for his hand and warmed it between both of hers. He had long fingers, like a pianist, and the large size of his hand made her own seem small.

"Let's start again," she said. "My name is Eugénie and you're in a wine cellar in the middle of a vineyard in Burgundy. My friends brought you here last night after your plane crashed. We're going to try to keep you safe. I've brought some wine that I hope will ease your pain."

With that said, Eugénie lifted the bottle to his lips, but did not try to lift his head. Two tiny streams of red trickled down his cheeks from the corners of his mouth, but he managed to swallow some of the wine.

"Who are you? And where are you from?" she tried again.

"My name's Joseph. Joseph Caillon, from Canada."

Eugénie was silent for a moment, astonished and deeply moved that someone would willingly take such an arduous journey from a place so far away, the other side of the world, to fight for the liberation of a dot on a map called Volnay. She closed her eyes and tried to imagine the splendour of that country of the north that Joseph Caillon sprang from, the crystal cold of its silent winters, the red and coppery leaves of its autumns, a place where every breath people took was free and no soldiers hunted anyone down.

It was a miracle that Joseph Caillon was here and she was sitting on the dry ground beside him, tucking an extra blanket around him to keep him warm and feeding him bits of bread soaked in sedated wine. It seemed to Eugénie that this man had come to her the way a dream does, unbidden and unexpected, impossible to avoid or turn away.

She was determined now to keep him alive.

June 1, 1944

Dear Julien,

Madeleine has completely taken over the task of sending you convoluted stories, so there are no more tricks in my words. Instead, here is a simple list of all the things that we are missing that perhaps you could pick up on your way home.

A stable mate for Jacques, whose old coat shines a glossy black due to Madeleine's brushing.

One new wheelbarrow tire, since ours is unaccountably flat.

A set of French classics for the education of Pierre, aged ten, who needs no further education from the street.

One new pot for Augustine, who rules the kitchen and who blackened her favourite in an herbal experiment.

A ribbon for Madeleine's hair because she asks for nothing.

A new pair of shoes for me as I've worn mine sorely down walking into the village to mail these letters that are written on the inside liners of packets of cigarettes and may dissipate like smoke before they ever reach you.

You. We are missing you, dearest brother, and surely you can manage to bring just you, and by so doing, make all of our other needs obsolete, so full will we be with the joy of your homecoming.

Always,
Eugénie

She did not include Gaston in her list, but Julien was clever and could read between unwritten lines.

AUGUSTINE STEEPED THE HERBS that Madeleine had collected in the forest in steaming water until all their goodness and healing power became distilled, a watery sap boiled down until it was finally transformed into thick syrup.

"My favourite story when I was a little girl," Madeleine rattled on, "was about my great grandmother who was very ugly and banished to the forest. She made potions from the leaves and plants just like these and they were said to be miraculous."

"Well we need a miracle now," Augustine replied. She poured her brew into an empty jar and loaded up the wheelbarrow with strips of cloth from a ripped up sheet and a basin of clean water.

"Try to get him to swallow some of that mixture," she ordered Eugénie. "You'll need to soak the head bandages before trying to remove them. Whatever he doesn't swallow, rub gently into his wounds."

"What if he's awake?" Eugénie asked.

"Can't hear a thing from the *cave*. Let him scream."

Eugénie blanched and Augustine peered into her face. "Those bandages have to be changed. Are you up to this? Just keep talking, rattle on about anything, like Madeleine does. It'll distract him."

Eugénie nodded, grasped the handles of the wheelbarrow, and crossed the vineyard with her burden.

Slowly she descended the stairs into the dimness of the cellar.

For three days, Joseph Caillon had wandered along the frontiers of death, at the end of which he drifted in and out of consciousness. Just as Eugénie had feared, he was awake now, turning his head toward her when he sensed her presence.

"Eugénie?" he called out in a voice rubbed raw by his struggle to go on living.

"I'm here, Joseph." She saw that his beard had thickened, even during her short absence from dusk to dawn. "I'm going to change your bandages."

He didn't say anything, but she saw the line of his jaw tighten and heard the shallowness of his breathing. She knelt beside him and began gently to sponge water onto his head with a soft strip of cloth. She remembered she was supposed to talk, but her mind was blank.

"How does your head feel?" she asked, lamely.

"Like molasses that doesn't want to be stirred."

"What's molasses?"

"It's a sweet, thick syrup."

"Oh. I've got some syrup here that Augustine made. Do you think you could swallow some?" Quickly, Eugénie slid a spoonful of the mixture into his mouth when he opened it to answer her.

He shuddered. "Tastes disgusting."

"Hush. You shouldn't be talking."

And since Eugénie hadn't the gift of Madeleine's storytelling, she bent to her gruesome task in silence.

When the bandages were saturated with water, she began to unwind them slowly, hearing him groan whenever she needed to lift his head. There were dozens of lacerations, as if he had smashed his head through a pane of glass. Some of the cuts were deep and vicious and clearly needed stitches. Some of them began to bleed when the bandages were disturbed.

Eugénie cleaned the cuts as best she could and dabbed them with Augustine's syrup, before applying fresh bandages. Beneath her hands, Joseph's eyes were tightly shut, the lids two dark smudges, the paleness of his face—a fine, strong face she could now see—an indication of his pain. For one terrible moment, she thought he looked like a marble sculpture lying on his own sarcophagus.

"I'm sorry," she whispered, parting his parched lips and feeding him spoonful after spoonful of Augustine's medicine until the jar was empty, then lifting a glass to his mouth so he could drink the taste away.

She held his hand until he slid away from her, back into unconsciousness, lost in the fog of nightmare that was the war, a war that had torn him away from his home and flung him out of the sky into this windowless cellar simply because he believed in something.

Eugénie contemplated her deepest fear: the postman trudging slowly toward her with a telegram in his hand, the dreaded words exploding in her mind. Maybe, she prayed, if she could save one life, another would be spared.

IT HAD RAINED HEAVILY MOST OF THE NIGHT. When Eugénie woke up, the rising sun was only a golden band at the eastern edge of a thickly clouded sky. She dressed quickly, eager to start work. Her grapes had just begun to grow and she wanted to see how they had withstood the storm. But first, she wanted to feed Joseph his breakfast.

She pulled on a sweater, tied chunks of bread and a bottle of broth into a kerchief, and started off across the field toward the *cave*. Half of the way there, she suddenly stopped and looked around her, amazed. Snow was falling from the sky in huge, fluttering flakes, a miracle of snow in June. Impossible. Birds, maybe. A great flock of strange, white birds were dipping and rising on the currents of the air. Then she heard the roar of the plane before she finally saw it, and stretched up a hand to catch at a piece of the white paper before it drifted to the ground. She read the words, shouted aloud, and fell to her knees.

The Allied Forces had landed in Normandy.

Her kerchief abandoned on the muddy field, she ran as fast as she could back to the house. She had forgotten how a rush of joy felt, the way it loosened her limbs, and lightened the pull of gravity so that she wanted to jump in the air and twirl in a circle and open her arms wide. She made such a racket that she woke everyone up, laughing at them as they stumbled into the kitchen, still rubbing sleep from their eyes.

In the midst of much hugging and exclaiming, Papa Vernoux arrived, bursting with news. "The battle has begun," he affirmed. "The largest sea and air offensive ever mounted. Yesterday, Radio London broadcasted eight hours of cryptic messages, each one a call to action for the Resistance. Everything and anything will be done to keep German troops from reaching Normandy. Stay close to the house. Avoid the village as best you can. The Germans are like lit sticks of dynamite now. I'll try to bring you food."

But Pierre could not be contained. He was almost through the door when Eugénie grabbed his sweater and pulled him back inside.

"Please, Eugénie," he whispered. "It's the best time to go. People will be feeling good and generous. Food for Joseph."

How could she have forgotten him, even for a moment? In her hesitation, Pierre slipped out of his sweater and out of her grasp and she stood and watched him jumping puddles as he crossed the road and headed toward Volnay.

IT WAS MIDDAY BY THE TIME Papa Vernoux left and Eugénie was free to visit the *cave*. She was nearly at the bottom of the stairs when she heard Joseph's raspy voice. "I can see you. I pulled up the bandage a bit, just to be sure I hadn't gone blind."

"Good," Eugénie smiled. "You must be feeling better."

"Are there two of you?"

"Ah, not that much better then. There's just one of me. I brought food. Broth and bread."

"Not that dreadful syrup, I hope."

"No. Chicken broth, a miracle cure for everything, according to Augustine. You can soak the bread in it, if it's too hard to chew, and I've brought an old sweater you can use as a pillow if it doesn't hurt too much to lift your head."

She'd only glanced at him when she arrived, busy setting out the food and folding up the sweater, but now, as she leaned toward him, she looked into his eyes. They were blue, cornflower blue, and they made her think of summer. They made his face look younger and more vulnerable. Suddenly he was a person to her, with dreams and plans and secrets, and not just an injured agent, remote from her.

"I have good news," Eugénie smiled. "The Allies have landed in Normandy. Perhaps you'll not have to hide much longer. Perhaps we'll all be free soon."

Joseph stopped eating for a moment, but he didn't look as surprised or as pleased as she thought he would.

"My mission," he explained. "I was to help co-ordinate the group in the Morvan with a group in Comblanchien just north of Beaune. I told as much as I could to the couple that pulled me from the plane, but I blacked out. If the Allies have landed, my mission is urgent. Please. Someone must go to Comblanchien and speak to the priest there. He's one of us and will know what to do."

"Don't worry. There are more people to help than I knew or guessed."

"People like you."

"Oh, I'm not a *résistant*. Not like Henri and the Legards. In fact, I've been selfish for most of the war, thinking about Julien and trying to save the vineyard. Trying to save myself, really."

"And yet here you are. Who's Julien?"

"My brother, my twin. So in a way there *are* two of me, but not in the way you thought when I came down the stairs. He's been in a prisoner of war camp for almost four years now."

"I'm sorry. How long have I been here? I've lost count of the days."

"Five days. Six, if you count the night you arrived."

"That explains it then."

Eugénie raised an eyebrow. Joseph shrugged and answered sheepishly, "I'm beginning to smell."

"Yes, you are," Eugénie laughed. "I'll bring water next time, and fresh clothes. You look about the same size as Julien. Do you think you can manage by yourself?"

"I'm in no position to be modest."

"No. But I still am. I'll send Augustine."

She asked him about his home then and he told her about growing up in Montreal with a French father and an English mother, and about the neon lights and bars and movie theatres of the city, and about the bold landscapes and mighty rivers beyond it.

"Are there vines?" Eugénie asked.

"There must be some, but nothing like the glory of vines here."

He rambled on about giant trees that would take the arms of four men to encircle, and golden seas of grain, but when he started describing pure white bears and eagles with four foot wing spans, she was sure he was losing his senses.

"I've tired you out," Eugénie interrupted. "Rest now."

She rose to leave, but he called out to her when she reached the stairs.

"Thank you, Eugénie. I think both of you are beautiful."
She felt a shyness she wasn't expecting and said goodbye.

June 6, 1944

Dear Julien,

This is a June like no other. Even sleepy Volnay is shaking itself awake, and the sky is filled with rare white birds bringing good news.

The grapes today are tiny, perfect orbs, drinking up the rain and growing plump. I walked among the vines, lost in a green cloud, and made a wish because this is the season when everything is as full of promise as a sun-filled, summer wedding.

Warmth, long soft evenings, birdsong, and pink roses. Pale gold wine with an aftertaste of verbena.

Maybe, just maybe, this will be a harvest like no other,

Always,
Eugénie

By dusk, Pierre had still not come home.

Augustine returned from her task of bathing and dressing Joseph in clean clothes, only to find Eugénie and Madeleine huddled over the kitchen table, frightening each other half to death by imagining all the misfortunes that could be visited upon the boy, from the extreme of arrest by the Gestapo to the simple mistake of losing track of time and everything in between.

Eugénie wrung her hands and said it was her fault for not stopping him from leaving, while Madeleine berated herself for not realizing how excited he was about the invasion when any fool could see the effect such news would have on a boy.

Augustine rapped her fist on the table and brought a halt to their moaning. "We've a bigger problem," she said gruffly. "I don't think we can leave Joseph in the *cave* much longer. The air in there is positively fetid. We need to move him."

"The stable?" Madeleine suggested.

"No. It's too open," Eugénie countered. "And besides there's the dogs to consider. You can't be out there quieting them all the time. We'll have to risk moving him in here."

The three women looked at each other, each sharing the same thought. Hard choices, dangerous choices—those were all that were left now.

Madeleine stood up. "I'm going to look for Pierre. Can you move Joseph without me, or should I ask Papa to help?"

"No," Eugénie urged. "Don't involve him. We can manage, can't we Augustine?"

The old woman nodded. "Just bring my lad home safely, Madeleine."

"I will." She blew them a kiss from the door and was gone.

Augustine smiled at Eugénie. "Mama and Papa Vernoux made no effort to prepare that child for life. That's why she knows no danger. She's blessed by the stars. But you and me? We need to pray for a night as black as pitch."

Eugénie tried to remember if she'd ever seen Augustine look frightened and hoped that maybe she, too, had been blessed by the stars.

BY MIDNIGHT, THOUGH, IT WAS EVIDENT that Augustine's prayer would not be answered. The moon was impossibly large and orange, and it lit up the fields, offering not the slightest cover and casting ominous shadows across the vines. Lovers or insomniacs who gazed out of their windows would be sure to spot any dark silhouettes under the bright moonbeams.

"We'll just crouch low among the vines," Augustine advised. "We can put him in the wheelbarrow and cover him with blankets on the way back."

When they slipped into the courtyard, two of the dogs lifted their noses, sniffing the air for the scent of food, but smelling only human sweat, they settled their heads back onto their paws and continued their dreams of rabbits and full bowls.

Eugénie reached the *cave* first, and called out softly to Joseph, but there was no response. She lit the lantern and knelt beside him, dismayed at what she saw. His skin was slick from the effort of breathing, his eyes without lustre, and his pupils dilated, which gave him a frightened, helpless look. The bandages on his head were once again bloodied.

"What happened, Augustine? He was so much better earlier. He even talked about his home," Eugénie cried.

"It sometimes happens, child. A rush of strength and then a bad turn. He'll not be able to help us, or put any weight on his good leg. Maybe we should ask Vernoux for his help, after all."

"No," Eugénie insisted, feeling a burst of strength of her own. "I won't put Madeleine's father in danger. We can do this."

The two women took up their positions, one at Joseph's head, one at his feet. They rocked him gently from side to side and then, on the count of three, swung him into the wheelbarrow.

His head and shoulders slumped forward and his splinted leg stuck out, stiff as the skeletal arm of a scarecrow. They pushed and pulled and bumped the wheelbarrow up the four stairs, each step up seeming like the scaling of a cliff.

When they reached the fresh, bright air of the moonlit night, Eugénie searched for a pulse at the side of Joseph's throat because, except for several faint grunts, the man had made no noise whatsoever and she was sure that they had killed him. She comprehended in that moment the cruelty of fate, which could lead a man along a terrible road before reaching this point of desperation and then simply abandon him to die in a wheelbarrow in a foreign land. Her anger at that injustice pumped adrenaline into her limbs and she ordered Augustine to cradle Joseph's head, while she grasped the handles of the wheelbarrow and pushed him over the bumpy field at a speed she wouldn't have thought possible. They dragged him across the kitchen floor and hefted him into a bed where he was finally shaken awake by a series of convulsions and panted like a tired dog.

Eugénie held him down by his shoulders until his body stopped shuddering and Augustine placed a warm poultice on his chest. After an hour, Joseph was breathing faintly, but shallowly.

"Go to bed, Augustine. You look exhausted. I'll sit with him and wait for Madeleine to come home."

It was three o'clock in the morning and both women were so drained that they hadn't enough heart left to admit to each other that Madeleine should have been home hours ago.

IT WAS PIERRE WHO WOKE EUGÉNIE up in her chair just as the dawn was beginning to shine through the windows.

She was so glad to see him that she threw her arms around him and hugged him while he squirmed in her embrace. "Where's Madeleine?" she asked when Pierre had managed to free himself.

"She's gone into the tunnels of the *caves.*"

"What?"

"It's okay. She sweet-talked Monsieur Drouhin into taking her. She's gone to look for Dr. Legard."

Eugénie looked over at Joseph, still breathing, still unconscious. "It may be too late," she sighed.

"Madeleine wouldn't take no for an answer."

"No. I don't suppose she would. And where have you been?"

"C'mon. I've got a surprise for you in the kitchen."

Pierre led her by the hand, his own very grubby she noticed, to the smiling face of Augustine taking inventory at the kitchen table of more food than Eugénie had seen in a months.

"There's a whole ham," Augustine marvelled. "I've already put that in the oven. Two pounds of real coffee, a pound of butter, a dozen bars of chocolate, and four rounds of bread, real bread made with white flour."

"How on earth—Pierre?" Eugénie gaped.

"I saw all the Germans were rushing out of town so I went to the big house. I figured it'd be empty and I slipped inside and found all this stuff in the icebox and shoved it into a pillow-case, but then I heard the jeep coming back so I hid under my old bed."

"You must have been terrified."

"Maybe a bit scared."

"A bit?"

"Okay. A lot. Anyway, I heard a German come into the room, I could see his boots, but he wasn't looking for me. Just yelling at somebody and he left the bedroom right away. I just figured I'd stay there until they left the house again or it got dark. But they never left and I waited all day and then Madeleine came."

"Madeleine? How did she find you?"

"She asked around the village and figured out where I'd most likely be. She climbed a tree and dropped into the courtyard. She said the radio was playing really loudly—I could hear it, too—and no one heard when she crept in by the kitchen window. We went out the same way, but when we reached the edge of the village, she said she was going across the fields to Pommard to find Monsieur Drouhin so she could look for the doctor in the tunnels and that's all I know."

"Well, Pierre, I think you deserve one of those bars of chocolate."

"That's okay. I already ate one when I was hiding," he grinned.

"How's Joseph?" Augustine asked Eugénie, but she just shook her head in reply.

"Well, it's been a day and a night of miracles. So have some breakfast. We've done all we can for now."

DR. LEGARD AND MADELEINE CAME UNDER COVER of night. While Madeleine looked invigorated by her adventure, the doctor looked sorely changed, his hair untrimmed and his beard thick and wolf like. Still, he had not lost the kindness of his touch, as he bent over Joseph and began to unwind his bandages. "Bring me hot water, Eugénie, and clean bandages," he requested.

His voice was calm, but when he looked at her, she could see his eyes were brimming with doubt.

Augustine began boiling water, while Eugénie set about destroying one of her mother's prized tablecloths and Madeleine coaxed Pierre to bed. The quiet in the house was as suspenseful as a held breath, so complete that each time Eugénie ripped a strip from the linen cloth, the tearing noise seemed unbearably loud and jarring. When finally she carried everything in to Dr. Legard, she grit her teeth and asked to help.

"No. I'm going to stitch him up. You'd better not watch."

She looked at Joseph, the wounds on his forehead and scalp looking violently red. She listened to the cadence of his breathing, trying to discern any irregularities, glad that his comatose state sheltered him from the grim reality of waking. Quietly, she crept away.

She drifted down to Pierre's bedroom, not knowing what to do with herself, and leaned against the open doorway. Madeleine was perched on the edge of the boy's bed.

"How does that story end?" Pierre asked Madeleine.

"Which one?"

"The one you and Eugénie were writing to Julien."

"Ah, well, I'm afraid the girl with the green mermaid hair was forsaken by her one true love and journeyed very far until she reached a vast sea and lost all the shine in her honeyed eyes. She dove right into that sea to drown her sorrows, but as she was sinking beneath the waves, a sailor saw her green hair spread all around, drifting and floating on the surface of the water, and because he thought it was seaweed, he pulled on it and pulled up the girl instead. She was so surprised to be alive, that she never felt sad again."

"That's a good story."

"Of course, I might change my mind."

"About the ending?"

"No. About who was really my one true love."

Even from the doorway, Eugénie could see that Pierre's smile was so broad that the rest of him almost disappeared behind it. Madeleine kissed the boy on the forehead and joined Eugénie, closing the door softly behind her. "Joseph?" she asked.

"I don't know. I'm afraid."

The two women went to the kitchen and sent Augustine to bed.

"We'll wait together and fix up some food for Dr. Legard." Madeleine suggested.

When the doctor finally emerged from Joseph's room, he was able to tell them between mouthfuls of ham sandwich and hot coffee that the man's unconsciousness was a blessing in disguise because it had allowed the swelling of the brain to recede and the stitching of his wounds to be done without further suffering.

"Keep him warm. Keep putting that foul-smelling salve on him, because I don't know why but it seems to be helping. And pray."

Madeleine led him past the dogs that had learned to mistrust the smell of men, and the good doctor melted into the darkness. No one seemed to notice that Eugénie was right behind him.

"Dr. Legard," she whispered. "I need your help. Joseph was to get a message to the priest in Comblanchien, something about uniting the group from the Morvan with the men in the village. I think it might ease him to know the message was delivered."

Dr. Legard shook his head. "I'm sorry, Eugénie, but I'm cut off from the Morvan now. I've no way of knowing if the message was delivered or not, and I can't take the risk of being abroad and arrested. I know too much. If you need to know for certain if the message was delivered—"

He left the rest of the sentence unspoken, but Eugénie, with a sense of dread, knew perfectly well what he meant.

AT DAWN, EUGÉNIE LACED UP HER STURDIEST BOOTS, packed a small basket with water and a bit of bread and cheese, and strode out to the fields. She'd been awake most of the night, checking on Joseph and planning her route. It was maybe eighteen kilometres to Comblanchien by road, but a much shorter distance over the fields. She'd told no one of her decision to deliver Joseph's message because she knew instinctively that no one thought of her as brave enough or rash enough to attempt such a journey. Augustine would roll her eyes in disbelief, Madeleine would insist on going in her stead, and Pierre would pout if he were told he couldn't come along. To them, and even to herself, she was just careful, cautious Eugénie with her head down among the vines, waiting for the war to pass her by, scarcely seen beyond the confines of the Latour estate or the village square.

But Joseph had changed all of that. Eugénie didn't give herself any credit for taking him into her home—anyone with a human heart would have done that. Yet she couldn't forget that he'd travelled from another world to offer his help, a distance that staggered her imagination. If he could do that, then surely she could take this long walk alone for him. And what danger could there be? Anyone could see she was perfectly harmless.

Faith filled her heart as she crossed field after field, hour after hour, climbing higher on a diagonal slant as she finally reached the upper slopes of the Côte d'Or where the finest wines sprang from the alchemy of sun and rain and earth. She began to recite their names as a kind of chant and wondered if the name "Latour" would one day rank among them. She stopped and shaded her eyes with her hand. Below her now, she could see the ramparts of the city of Beaune, and flying above them half a dozen German swastika flags. She turned her back on them and kept walking.

She wished she'd remembered to wear a hat. She could feel her skin burning under the sun. A bead of sweat trickled down between her breasts and her clothes felt itchy. Where was everyone? The fields were strangely empty. She'd seen a grandfather huddled down among the vines with a small boy, no doubt giving him his first lesson of the mystery of the vines, but only the odd worker here and there. She didn't know the time, but the sun was high so perhaps the French were eating what passed for lunch these days in shady courtyards.

She found a tree to settle under and opened her basket, drinking half the water in one gulp. *If I eat all the food now*, she thought, *I can use the napkin as a scarf to cover my head.* But that would leave her nothing for the journey home. Well, perhaps the priest could spare some food. The priest. With a sudden chill, she realized she didn't even know his name. Comblanchien was small, she reminded herself—there'd only be one priest. What if he wasn't there? What if he travelled from village to village? What day was it anyway?

Eugénie stood up abruptly and stuffed everything back into her basket. If she stayed still, she would drive herself crazy thinking of all that could go wrong. *Just keep moving*, she told herself. *Keep walking.*

After an hour, she passed by the beauty of Aloxe-Corton, the elegant white house shining in the sun, roof tiles flashing red and gold. She knew the Germans had requisitioned the estate, so she dipped her head low. She was just a slim figure, moving in an unhurried way, framed by the forests and the vineyards under an immense sky in the quiet of the French countryside.

Eventually she reached the huddle of houses that was the village of Comblanchien, with only a few stray cats lounging about in the sun to greet her. Again, she felt that eerie sense of emptiness that she had noticed in the fields and found again in the village lanes and square. She decided not to take that emptiness as an omen of ill fortune, and marched up to the church, as sturdy, unadorned, and functional a building as the one she knew so well in Volnay.

She pushed at the door and found it open. Inside the air was cool, scented by candles that formed little pools of light at the feet of carved saints, the perpetual endowers of comfort for those who believed in them. The coolness was a welcome relief to Eugénie after the fierceness of the sun, and she sat down in the first pew she came to, wondering if the priest would appear soon, or if he lived nearby, or if he were even in the village at all. She saw now that her plan had been ill conceived and impetuous, and the only thing to be done was to sit and wait, and perhaps offer a prayer or two to those blank eyed saints.

She calculated that more than an hour had passed when the door was finally opened and a startled voice from behind her finally roused her from alternating spells of frustration and self-recrimination over her own folly.

"What's your name? And what's brought you here?" the priest asked. "I'm Father Maurice."

The priest was tall and gaunt-looking, with a day's beard and a fierce expression.

"I'm Eugénie and I've brought a message from Joseph. His plane crashed and some people brought him to me, and now I've come to you. He said you would know what to do."

To Eugénie's shock, the priest swore, a long string of some of the filthiest words she had ever heard. When he finally stopped cursing, he almost laughed at the look of horror on Eugénie's face. "I'm not really a priest," he confessed. "I don't believe in some reward in the sky. The point is to fight for your rights on earth. Where are you from and how did you get here?"

"I'm from Volnay. I walked across the fields."

The priest—the man in priest's robes—swore again.

"Please," Eugénie held up a hand. "I've heard enough of that."

The man shrugged. "Sorry, but you've shocked me, too. Look, we have to get out of here."

"What's happened? Why is it so quiet in the village?"

"There's no time for questions. Can you ride a bicycle?"

Eugénie nodded, suddenly afraid.

"Wait here. When you hear a bicycle bell, go out by the back door of the church. I'll travel to Volnay with you."

"But—"

"Please. Just do as I say."

There was a swirl of black cassock and then the man was gone. Eugénie walked slowly towards the back of the church, behind the altar where she'd never been in her whole life. She felt like she was doing something unholy, but fear kept her searching behind a curtain and down a narrow hallway until she found the back door. She leaned her head against it and crossed herself, both to apologize for the path she'd just taken and to protect her on the path that lay beyond.

She heard the bell and opened the door, the light from a low sun almost blinding her after the shadows of the church. Through squinting eyes, she saw two bikes and a man, no longer a priest, in the work clothes of a vintner.

"Get on," he ordered. "We'll ride side by side. Not too fast, mind, but steady. Don't look back. If we're stopped, I'll do the talking. Just follow my lead."

Eugénie put her head down and pedalled.

Two hours later, the aches and pains in her legs had blossomed into full-blown agony. She had never in her life been so grateful to see Volnay. As they reached the square, the man dismounted.

"This is where I stop," he said. "I'll need to take your bicycle. Can you make it home from here?"

"Yes."

"Tell me, is the man you call Joseph alive?"

"I don't know. He was when I left this morning."

"Well I hope he lives long enough to be grateful to you for delivering his message. You needn't tell him that it came too late."

He turned away from her, pushing the bicycles, one on each side of his body.

Eugénie just stood and watched him, hurt and angry and astonished to see him knock at Madame Valleray's door.

JOSEPH DID NOT DIE THAT NIGHT, or the next.

On the third morning after her journey, Eugénie was standing at the kitchen sink, when Madame Valleray burst through the front door of the house without even knocking.

"Sweet Jesus. Mary, Mother of God," she gasped. "Comblanchien's been razed to the ground."

The glass Eugénie was holding crashed on the floor.

Augustine quickly slipped out of Joseph's room, closing the door behind her. From somewhere, maybe thin air, Madeleine appeared at Eugénie's shoulder.

"What happened?" Augustine demanded, reaching for a chair and guiding Madame Valleray into it.

The old woman flapped her hands and shook her head and crossed herself repeatedly before spilling out her news in a jumble of words: "Eight men shot. Oh, sweet Jesus. Who knows how many others rounded up for deportation? Women and children ran into the fields. Hid among the vines. Houses burned. They even burned the church to the ground."

"SS or soldiers?" Augustine prodded.

"Oh those devils all in black, as black as their hearts. A reprisal, the devils said."

"A reprisal for what?" Augustine persisted.

"One of their own. Shot in the back only two days ago. They claim someone in the village did it."

Eugénie slumped, and might have slumped to the floor had Madeleine not been there to hold her up. She remembered the unnatural quiet of the countryside and the village, what she knew now had been the uneasy quiet before a storm, the collective pent-up breath of the terrified, waiting for the terror to strike, for the fist to pound. Why hadn't they run or hidden sooner?

She knew one man who had run, who had known the terror would strike. Was he the very man who had pulled the fateful trigger, unleashing the fury of revenge against the innocents of Comblanchien? Or was he her saviour? Or both?

Augustine brought water to Madame Valleray and rubbed her shoulders, and pretended to ignore the broken glass on the floor and the way the blood had drained from Eugénie's face. "And how do you know all this, Madame Valleray?" she asked gently.

"Oh, the whole village knows. We're all wondering if Volnay will be next. A friend of Armand's from the seminary came to visit just a day before it all happened. He lived in Comblanchien and might have been shot himself."

"A priest?" Eugénie managed to ask.

"No. He dropped out, but he's smart all right. He said he could smell trouble and he headed out for the Morvan just in time. It's a miracle, I say. It's God protecting his own."

Eugénie didn't suppose there was anything miraculous about it. The man had said that her message had come too late. The German officer had already been shot, and the man had known that, too.

SOON AFTER EUGÉNIE'S POINTLESS JOURNEY, the bombing began. Day after day, planes roared overhead on their way to Chalon-sur-Saône, thirty kilometres to the south. They pounded the port and the bridges and lit up the sky with orange balls of flame. Pierre whooped with joy and raised a celebratory fist to the sky whenever the planes swooped over, but Madeleine shuddered and prayed she would never be the target of such perfect instruments of chaos and destruction.

Eugénie, as always, worked in the fields, but whenever she wasn't with the vines, she was with Joseph. His periods of lucidity were growing longer, sometimes lasting several days, before he would begin to ramble and lose sense of things. She read to him and told him stories of her childhood. She washed his face and changed his bandages and saw his blue eyes widen when he saw Madeleine for the first time.

Two weeks after the Allied landing, France suffered the worst storm it had seen in four decades. Madeleine and Eugénie were sitting alone at the kitchen table, talking as they often did while the rest of the house slept. The air rumbled, low and deep, predicting the approach of thunder.

Thinking of the vines, Eugénie ran to the window. The thunder cracked directly overhead, followed immediately by a flash of

light that illuminated the whole vineyard. Spellbound, Eugénie
watched as the sky burst into a kind of white fire. She staggered
back, blinded by it and then suddenly deafened by a crack so
loud it seemed the very earth itself were splitting open. The
rain pelted down, lashing the windows, and sweeping away
the nests of the doves in gushing streams of water.

Eugénie backed away from the window, beaten. She could
do nothing, save nothing. She slumped in her chair and hardly
noticed when Madeleine hugged her and rubbed her shoulders. Eugénie just clutched the edge of the table as if she were
clinging to wreckage, while everything she loved and dreamt
for spun away from her in a swirling torrent.

"Tell me a story," Madeleine urged.

Eugénie didn't even respond.

"Try, Eugénie. I promise it will help."

Eugénie raised her head in a daze. Unbidden, she suddenly
remembered a fairy tale that Julien used to tease her with as a
child about a man who cheated Death and so saved his lady
love. Just as Death stretched out his fingers to snatch up the
maiden, the hero substituted a fat chicken in her place. Death
roared, a scorching howl filled with singed feathers, but threatened to be back.

Julien loved the story for the hero's cleverness, but Eugénie
always covered her ears, imagining that howl and Death's
breath of fire that could burn a chicken alive. You couldn't
cheat Death completely, not even in a fairy tale. That was the
real world. That was the story she'd been told over and over
again. She didn't think there could ever be any different ending.

"I don't know any stories," she said, without intonation,
without hope.

"Then tell me *your* story," Madeleine demanded.

Eugénie looked into Madeleine's eyes and saw permission
there. She looked out at the night, and the wildness of the
storm seemed to shake something loose inside her and so she
told the story that no one else knew.

"It was so hot that August afternoon. I came home from the village and I saw that the stable door was unlatched and when I walked inside, I stepped on something—broken glass—and I knew something was terribly wrong. It was so dark inside because the day was so bright. I saw a shadow move. Gaston. It was Gaston. He staggered towards me and he was bleeding. There was blood all over his face.

"I ran to help him, but he pushed me away, swearing. I fell down and he loomed over me and said 'I'll kill her. I'm going to kill that crazy bitch.' And he kicked me because I was pulling on his leg to try to stop him from going anywhere. Jacques was wild. I thought he was going to smash his stall to pieces and his eyes were rolling in his head. I screamed at Gaston to stop and he picked me up and started shaking me by the shoulders. And I thought there's only one way to end this. Fast. And that's how it happened. Fast. He turned his back on me and I picked up the rake and hit him again and again until he fell and stopped moving.

"Everything seemed to blur and turn black. I heard the bats' wings and they frightened me and I ran back to the house."

"What happened then?" Madeleine whispered.

"Then? There was no then. He was dead. I murdered my own brother."

"What did you do with his body, Eugénie?"

"I don't know. I still don't know. I remember being delirious that night, thinking there was something left undone, but I couldn't bring myself to go back into the stable. When I realized a day later you weren't coming back, I knew Jacques would starve without me so I went in to feed him with my eyes shut tight. But when I opened them, Gaston wasn't there. The body disappeared. But I know that I killed him and that there isn't enough forgiveness in the world to save me."

That night Eugénie cried for the first time, covering her face with her blankets to suffocate her grief. Madeleine heard her and came to soothe her and wipe away her tears.

"I killed Gaston first, Eugénie. That's the only part of the story you need to remember. Since we killed him together, we'll share the burden together and, in time, it will seem lighter."

But that night there was no comforting Eugénie, even with such a fabulous tale, so Madeleine simply rocked her in her arms, lulling her to sleep, and that is where dawn and Augustine found them, curled up together like two abandoned kittens from Madeleine's menagerie.

The storm raged for three days, stunning the countryside. When it was over, Eugénie waded out to the smashed vines and sank up to her ankles in mud.

June 24, 1944

Dear Julien,

Your words so often ended my sentences. Your dreams became my dreams. We were twinned before birth, but Mama always said you came first and I followed.

Burgundy, this glorious place, is in my blood—the restless skies, the slant of light across the vines, the deep scent and steady beating rhythm of the land. I am still here, but I am not the same Eugénie who kissed you goodbye. You were not here and I had to wonder if you were even still alive, and I had to find my own way.

Apart, we have travelled to places so foreign the other cannot know them or follow. Never mind. I've learned that memory is fragile and that what we do not wish to remember passes from it quickly and is replaced by pages from a different story which allows us to go on living. This war is many wars, and yours is different from mine, and mine has untwinned me, though I am still here, loving you.

Always,
Eugénie

MAYBE IT WAS THE OLD-FASHIONED and mysterious herbal remedies, or the skill of Dr. Legard, or just the whim of the gods, but Joseph did not die. By the end of August, he was up and walking about, though his right leg did not quite keep pace with his left and he tired after a few hours. He began to strain at his confinement and was conscious of the fact that his presence was a loaded gun pointed at the inhabitants of the Latour farmhouse.

"I must go," he said to Eugénie. "I couldn't live with myself if anything happened to you."

"You're too weak," she replied. "Stay."

"Tell me about the tunnels under the *caves*," he asked Madeleine.

"Entering them is like being swallowed by a huge black mouth. You don't want to go there," she warned.

"Can you get word to the partisans in the Morvan?" he asked Pierre.

"No. Auntie would thrash me if I tried to go there, and you too, if you weren't so big."

So Joseph stayed while the bombing and shelling continued to pound Chalon-sur-Saône all summer long, night after night, making the dishes clatter and the dogs howl and the German soldiers race up and down the dusty roads in their military trucks. Sometimes, Eugénie would hear isolated gun shots and wonder if Léa was the shooter or the shot at, and she would look at Madeleine, who was a magnet for other people's problems, and know she was imagining irreversible disasters because all her stories now were about spring and love, as if to keep everyone posted about the fact that there was still hope and goodness in the world.

During the night of September 6th, Eugénie was awakened by something she had not heard for months: silence.

The doves had returned after the June storm and by dawn, Eugénie, who had remained still for hours for fear that the slightest movement would shatter the blessed quiet, swore she could hear the doves cooing. There was no doubt about it. The bombing had ceased.

She was sitting at the kitchen table with Augustine and Joseph, eating breakfast and thinking about the meagre harvest that awaited her, when Madeleine and Pierre came flying through the front door.

"Come on. Hurry," they shouted and disappeared again as quickly as they had come.

Augustine grabbed a frying pan in case she had need of a weapon, but Eugénie heard the grinding of gears and motors, and the blare of horns in the distance and grabbed Joseph's hand instead.

"Come with me," she urged. "I thought this might happen last night when the bombing stopped."

The five friends stood at the edge of the road that skirted the Latour estate and watched in amazement as American jeeps filled with American soldiers with American grins advanced slowly but unmistakably towards Pommard and Beaune.

Madeleine and Pierre were the first to jump onto a jeep's running board, but soon villagers were pouring down the hill from Volnay and the Americans were happy to take on passengers. One jeep stopped to give old Augustine a place of honour on the front seat, and she presented the driver with her frying pan and a kiss on the cheek. Joseph lifted Eugénie onto the back of a truck and reached for the open hands that hauled him up behind her.

The procession entered Beaune to the jubilant sound of church bells and people singing at the top of their lungs, beside themselves with joy. Amid the jumble of voices and dancing, Eugénie watched as a group of soldiers unwound a large roll of white fabric on the paving stones in front of the church and made a cross with it, a sign to let Allied planes know Beaune had been liberated.

French flags, buried for years in attics and trunks, blossomed in windows all through the town, and the wine—the best wine, carefully secreted away in bottles dusted with cobwebs—flowed freely. For Burgundians that was the taste of victory that their tongues would never forget, the berries and black currents of the Beaujolais, the ripe pears and apples of the Sancerres, the golden Meursaults with overtones of honey and almonds.

Eugénie and Joseph were swept along by the happy avalanche, waving once to Pierre as they swirled by, laughing to see that his mouth was full of American chewing gum.

Then, suddenly, there was a moment of stillness amid the commotion and the crowds seemed to part to behold a beautiful sight: two women, the black hair and the golden tangled together as they embraced. Léa and Madeleine had found each other like two stars drawn to each other's orbit.

When they finally let go of each other, their faces were radiant.

Léa hugged Eugénie. "Well done," she whispered. "You kept him alive. I never thought he'd make it."

"Meet Joseph Caillon," Eugénie smiled, and Léa kissed him to welcome him back to life.

"Come with me," she shouted and everyone was on the move again. She led them along through the crowd, ducking well-wishers and soldiers wanting to dance with French girls, and finally stopped at a pale pink door on the Rue Paradis.

She executed a complicated series of knocks and the door opened. Someone was holding a torch up, illuminating the darkness beyond the doorway, but a second shadow moved forward and Dr. Legard stepped into his daughter's arms.

Eugénie stared upwards into that band of torchlight and saw particles of dust caught and falling, appearing as tiny bursts of light and then dissolving, exactly the way stars shoot across the sky. Despite her doubt of miracles, she realized then that the world is full of wonderment even on the tiniest scale, if the mind is open to seeing it. That effervescent dust was as beautiful as anything she had ever seen, as beautiful as a vine, or a healthy man, or a loyal friend, but then, when she saw it, she was in love and as happy as any human being can be.

THE NEXT MORNING, AUGUSTINE AND PIERRE set off to explore the big house. Pierre was hoping he might find a cache of food forgotten by the Germans in their rush to retreat, but Augustine was certain the Germans would have taken not only the food, but also the silver they'd used to eat it. She was prepared to catalogue a list of missing furniture, paintings and jewellery for Monsieur Benoir.

Since Madeleine had left at dawn to visit Léa, Eugénie busied herself making breakfast for Joseph, who sat at the kitchen table and watched her every move, clutching the last cup of real coffee in his hands and rehearsing everything he wanted to say, frustrated that he could not think of a single way to begin.

Eugénie finally sat down across from him and looked him in the eye. "When is the jeep coming?"

"You know?"

"I know the war is over for me, but not for you. Where will you go?"

"The Americans will arrange safe passage to England. After that, I'm not sure. Eugénie, I—"

She reached across the table and placed a finger over his lips. "Let's not say goodbye here. Follow me."

She led him into the rows of vines, damaged by the storm but not dead, and spread her arms wide.

"This is my inheritance," she said. "And it will be my legacy. Across the road there are more vines, and over those hills, still more. I love the regularity of the planting—it feels familiar and predictable, but it drove my younger brother mad. He could never see that the fickleness of the weather was nature's perfect counterpoint to predictability, and he couldn't understand that every harvest is a surprise, no two ever exactly alike. This year's wine will be thin and watery, but legend promises that Our Lady of the Vines sends a poor crop when war starts and a festive one to mark its end. So maybe 1945 will be a glorious harvest. There's something I need to tell you about my brother, Gaston."

"I already know," Joseph interrupted.

He read the look of puzzlement and anxiety on her face and continued quickly. "The storm woke me and I heard you and Madeleine talking in the kitchen. Your brother wasn't a good man."

"That's beside the point."

"Is it? Because I don't believe you would ever hurt a living creature in this world unless you were pushed too far for too long, and convinced a beloved friend was in danger. Let him go now, let go and live your life."

She turned away from him, but he drew her back and framed her face in his hands and kissed her again and again.

"Will you wait for me, Eugénie?" he asked.

"No," she laughed. "I'm done with waiting. But if you come back, you'll find me here among the vines and I'll be glad to see you."

She laid her head on his shoulder and they held hands until they heard the jeep approaching. She waved him goodbye and walked slowly back to the kitchen. She did not watch the jeep drive away, nor did she glance at the empty road.

As IT HAPPENED, EUGÉNIE WAS NOT AT HOME when Julien returned. It was Madeleine, standing where the golden, wild grass still grew long, bending in the September wind, who looked down the road and saw a tall, too thin man, wearing pants patched at the knees, a sweater that hung from his frame, and four years of suffering across his shoulders.

She did not make the slightest movement until he was close enough for her to extend a hand to him and look into the face that was already dear to her. "Welcome home, Julien."

"You must be Madeleine." His voice was deep and slow as the bottom of a river. "Tell me, how does the story end?"

Madeleine just smiled and fell into the look in his eyes. She slipped her arm under his, and he leaned against her strength as she guided him to the house.

"We're very good at rehabilitation," she assured him. "Augustine brews a medicine that will either knock you out or get your blood rushing. Eugénie has a gentle touch, and Pierre and I provide food and entertainment, but first you must sleep for several days and, when you wake up, you'll see the beloved face of your sister, who has ached for your return and will surely shout for joy when she learns that you've come back to her. Here we are. Don't mind the dogs—they won't hurt you. Go ahead, open the door."

Julien crossed the threshold. He looked all around with tears streaming down his face. He entered every room, and touched the surfaces of the walls and the furniture, while Madeleine prepared a steaming bath and then helped him undress without the slightest embarrassment, as if he were a child.

When he was clean and fed, he fell into the first proper bed he'd seen in years.

"I can't believe it. I can't believe you," he said, already falling into a sleep that would have no dreams because they had all come true, at last.

"You'll get over that," Madeleine promised.

ON A SHINING DECEMBER MORNING with a clear, brittle edge, Léa came to visit her friends and found them in the stable with Jacques.

"I've brought you a surprise," she announced. "All the way from Paris."

Eugénie smiled to see the pretty girl she remembered from better harvests, but Madeleine saw a new Simone, a woman no longer needing to camouflage her true self like those creatures whose colour automatically adapts to whatever surroundings they happen to be in. Her gaze was more direct, more confident. Whatever mirrors had been held up to her in Paris had done her good.

For her part, Simone was willing to concede that Madeleine was not contaminated by clairvoyance, just afflicted with an unsettling clarity of vision. She found she was able to breathe easily in her presence because she was no longer burdened by secrets.

"Father has come to close up the house with Augustine's help," she explained. "After what happened there, he wants nothing more to do with it. Not that there's anything of value left. The Germans took whatever wasn't nailed down.

"What I've really come to tell you is that the family spent months searching for my mother, but every door we tried had already slammed shut. We finally learned only two weeks ago that she'd been taken to a place called Ravensbrück where she was executed on the very day she arrived. The way she died shocked us, but it was easier than imagining a prolonged suffering."

"I'm so sorry, Simone," Madeleine sighed.

"Your mother was brave," Léa added. "The village will not forget her. What will your father do now?"

"He'll shift his Burgundy office to Pommard, but we'll return to Paris. Augustine wants to come home, but I think Pierre would like to stay and his parents have agreed, if it's all right with you. There's still not much to eat in Paris."

"He's welcome for as long as he wants," Eugénie smiled. "He's grown up during the war—almost a man now—and he's a big help to Julien and me."

"Oh, yes. I heard that Julien had returned," Simone said. "And what of Gaston?"

For a moment, it seemed to Simone that the warm faces of her friends were suddenly sculpted in ice. Léa and Eugénie studied the ground, but Madeleine held Simone's gaze.

"I wish he'd gone to Paris with you. He might have been happy there," she said.

"We were never really engaged," Simone confessed. "It was just a plan to help him escape Volnay. Papa would have compensated you, Eugénie, for his lost labour. Still, it's a mystery that he never showed up, even though my mother told me I was a fool to think he would. Perhaps she knew him better than I did."

The three women looked at each other disconcertedly, while Simone's unwitting truth floated in the air, as fragile as a sigh. For what seemed an infinite time, but was only seconds, they stood immobile adjusting to the weight of their secrets. What is never spoken, never ceases being. It only grows larger.

Eugénie stepped forward. "I never understood Gaston. His going is my fault."

She was about to say more, but Simone's attention had already shifted to the sound of an approaching car. "Oh, that'll be Papa. I must go. Come to visit. Come to Paris. We've lots of room."

Before any of the others could speak, Simone had already turned away, was already running back to her reclaimed Paris that was altered forever, but becoming more and more like she wished it could be.

The three women left behind in the courtyard waved and watched Monsieur Benoir's car disappear up the road. The low, slanting sun cast long shadows and Eugénie shivered in the cool air.

"Are we never going to tell her the truth?" she demanded. "I feel like he's listening to me all the time, locked in silence, waiting for me to tell the truth. I killed him."

Léa was astounded. "You killed him? But I thought—"

Madeleine put her arm around Eugénie. "I killed him, too. I left him for dead. What did you do with the body, Léa?"

"It's a long story."

"I imagine. But we've waited a long time."

She held out her hand. Léa took it, and the three women settled themselves in the shade under the linden tree.

Amid the millions of words Léa knew, she couldn't think of one that would help her begin. The single drop of water that causes the dam to break cannot be traced, and this felt like releasing a flood.

"I ... I ... I..." she stuttered.

"You," Madeleine nodded, "entered the barn and you found Gaston dead, and then?"

"I knew immediately that he was dead, bashed about the head. There was broken glass. I'd expected that, but not the rake. The rake, well the rake had obviously been used to hit him, and I thought you, Maddy, had probably just blocked that part out.

"I thought of running to my father for help, but I didn't want to get him in trouble, and I knew he was sitting with old Grenelle's body. That's when I knew what to do. I dragged Gaston to the wheelbarrow and pushed and prodded until I got him into it. I waited until it was dark. I could see bats flitting about. When I peeked around the stable door, I could see Eugénie's bicycle was leaning against the house, but no light was visible through the blackout curtains.

"I pushed the wheelbarrow all the way to the old graveyard behind the chapel, and then I ran back for the rake, and a shovel, and a rope. The grave for Grenelle was already dug. All I had to do was dig a little deeper, tip Gaston into the grave, and cover him up."

Léa stopped talking. Her eyes were closed, but she was seeing herself as she'd been that night, grim and horrified by what had to be done. Her breath came in pants and her hands shook.

Madeleine went to her side and began to stroke her hair to soothe her. Eugénie couldn't move.

"I thought it would be easy," Léa finally resumed, "but it wasn't. Every sound was magnified—the owls flapping in the night, the thud of the body as it hit the dirt, the scrape of the shovel. When I turned him over, his eyes were open, and for one horrible moment it felt like he was laughing at me. I closed his eyes. I hadn't thought to bring a cloth or a blanket to cover him, so I took off my sweater and placed it over his face. Then I smoothed out the dirt as best I could with the rake and threw the tools back up onto the ground.

"I'd tied one end of the rope to a gravestone, and the other end around my waist so that I could climb out. But my hands were sweaty and dirty and I kept falling back. I swear the night was no longer a shape I recognized. It was a black river pulling me under. I had to hold on so tightly.

"When I finally crawled out, I was filthy and panting like a dog. I just lay there and gazed up at the stars, and thought of you, Maddy, star-gazing from the tree in your yard. I took everything back to the barn and washed the tools in the horse trough, and spread some fresh hay around. And I carried Achilles back home and buried him.

"The next day, I went to Grenelle's funeral. I was terrified, sure Gaston would be discovered, but no one noticed a thing. Grenelle's coffin was lowered on top of him while the whole village watched.

"I know I did a dreadful thing. I did it for Maddy, Eugénie, because I thought she'd killed him in self-defence. I hope you can forgive me."

"Forgive you? You saved me. Burying Gaston was the right ... the decent thing to do. I wanted him to disappear, to do no more harm. You've put his ghost to rest and given me peace."

Madeleine rose then and led her friends along the same path that Léa had taken that terrifying night across the field to the chapel burial ground, where they stood looking down solemnly at old Grenelle's grave.

"Grenelle was a lovely old man," Léa said. "I don't think he minds the company. Later in the war, Papa and I buried a partisan, Henri's friend, on top of him because the headstone hadn't yet been placed. This is a triple grave now. I promise you, it will be blessed."

Eugénie looked down at the grave. "Gaston," she said. Only his name, part prayer, part regret, part goodbye.

THE THREE WOMEN NEVER SPOKE AGAIN about what had happened that August afternoon and night of 1943, and they never betrayed each other. They shared an unbreakable bond, forged by a secret both terrible and profound.

Time passed. Peace returned to Burgundy. Madeleine and Léa and Eugénie swung back into the rhythm of village life they'd known all their lives. Church bells rang out across the land for each of their weddings, and they named their children after each other. Rain continued to fall from the clouds, the sun lit up the sky, and the vines grew. The taste of wine lingered on their tongues and their children laughed. It was more than enough for them. In their hearts, it was a kind of miracle, and they infused the rest of their days with such love that they surely earned the grace of forgiveness.

ACKNOWLEDGEMENTS

I am grateful to my friends and family for their ongoing encouragement, especially Fran Cohen who is my constant reader and Arthur Haberman who is my constant everything.

My deep thanks also to the artist, Anne Virlange, and to everyone at Inanna Publications for their support, especially Luciana Ricciutelli for her perceptive editing and her kindness of spirit.

This novel is a tribute to halcyon time spent in Burgundy, France, and the magic it inspired.

Photo: Jake Whitla

Jan Rehner retired as University Professor from the Writing Department at York University. Her novel, *Just Murder*, won the 2004 Arthur Ellis Award for Best First Crime Novel in Canada. Her second novel, *On Pain of Death*, a historical narrative set in World War II France, won a bronze medallion from the IPPY group of independent publishers (2008). Her third novel, *Missing Matisse* (2011), longlisted for the ReLit Awards, combines a search for a lost Matisse painting with a fictionalized account of Matisse's famed model, Lydia Delectorskaya. Jan has visited France many times and continues to live in Toronto.